Presents

Great news! From this month onward, Harlequin Presents® is offering you more!

Now, when you go to your local bookstore, you'll find that you have *eight* Harlequin Presents® titles to choose from—more of your favorite authors, more of the stories you love.

To help you make your selection from our July books, here are the fabulous titles that are available: *Prince of the Desert* by Penny Jordan—hot desert nights! *The Scorsolini Marriage Bargain* by Lucy Monroe—the final part of an unforgettable royal trilogy! *Naked in His Arms* by Sandra Marton—the third Knight Brothers story and a sensationally sensual read to boot! *The Secret Baby Revenge* by Emma Darcy—a passionate Latin lover and a shocking secret from his past! *At the Greek Tycoon's Bidding* by Cathy Williams—an ordinary girl and the most gorgeous Greek millionaire! *The Italian's Convenient Wife* by Catherine Spencer—passion, tears and joy as a marriage is announced! *The Jet-Set Seduction* by Sandra Field—fasten your seat belt and prepare to be whisked away to glamorous foreign locations! *Mistress on Demand* by Maggie Cox—he's rich, ruthless and really...irresistible!

Remember, in July, Harlequin Presents® promises more reading pleasure. Enjoy!

MISTRESS
TO A
MILLIONAIRE

*She's his in the bedroom,
but he can't buy her love…*

Showered with diamonds, draped in
exquisite lingerie, whisked around the
world in the lap of luxury…

The ultimate fantasy becomes a reality.

Live the dream with more
MISTRESS TO A MILLIONAIRE titles
by your favorite authors.

Coming in September:
Mistress for a Weekend
by Susan Napier
#2569

Available only in Harlequin Presents®

Maggie Cox
MISTRESS ON DEMAND

MISTRESS
TO A
MILLIONAIRE

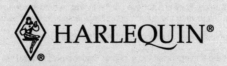

TORONTO • NEW YORK • LONDON
AMSTERDAM • PARIS • SYDNEY • HAMBURG
STOCKHOLM • ATHENS • TOKYO • MILAN • MADRID
PRAGUE • WARSAW • BUDAPEST • AUCKLAND

ISBN-13: 978-0-373-12554-8
ISBN-10:   0-373-12554-2

MISTRESS ON DEMAND

First North American Publication 2006.

www.eHarlequin.com

Printed in U.S.A.

All about the author…
Maggie Cox

MAGGIE COX loved to write almost as soon as
she learned to read. Her favorite occupation was
daydreaming and making up stories in her head;
this particular pastime stayed with her through all
the years of growing up, starting work, marrying
and raising a family. No matter what was going
on in her life, whether joy, happiness, struggle or
disappointment, she'd go to bed each night and
lose herself in her imagination.

For many years she secretly filled exercise books
and then her word processor with her writing,
never showing anyone what she wrote. It wasn't
until she met her second husband, and the "love
of her life," that she was persuaded to start sharing
those stories with a publisher. Maggie settled on
Harlequin as she has loved reading romance novels
since she was a teenager. After several rejections,
the letters that were sent back from the publisher
started to become more and more positive and
encouraging, and in July 2002 she sold her first book.

The fact that she is a published author is truly a
dream come true; however, each book she writes
is still a journey in "courage and hope" and a quest
to learn and grow and be "the best writer she can."
Her advice to aspiring authors is: "Don't give up at
the first hurdle, or even the second, third or fourth,
but keep on keeping on until your dream is realized,
because if you are truly passionate about writing and
learning the craft, as Paulo Coelho states in his book
The Alchemist, 'the universe will conspire to help
you make it a reality.'"

CHAPTER ONE

SOPHIE had woken up with an awful presentiment that the day wouldn't go well. From the moment she'd squirted toothpaste all down the front of her pyjama top, to the near disaster when she'd just narrowly escaped spilling a whole mug of coffee down the front of the 'posh' frock she was reluctantly wearing to her friend Diana's wedding, her nerves had been jangled. Okay, so she didn't like weddings—*hated* them, in fact, but Diana was her closest female friend, and after a tumultuous year when her volatile relationship with Freddie was on one minute, then off the next, the least Sophie could do was show up and bear witness to the occasion.

But her luck, if she was going to be blessed with any at all today—and Sophie was beginning to think that she wasn't—just seemed to get worse and worse. She'd made three-quarters of the journey to the register office in her car when there'd been an awful spluttering hiss from the engine, then a pop, then...*nothing*, as it had finally given up the ghost and come to an undignified end by the side of the road. Sophie had had no alternative but to grab her coat and start walking to the register office. There was nobody she could ring for help because she wasn't covered for breakdown and, besides, *wouldn't you know it?* she'd left her mobile phone on the hall table *along with her purse* as she'd rushed out through the door. So she hadn't even been able to get a taxi.

Now, as she hurried across the grey London pavements grimly clutching her umbrella because it had been raining all morning, and was *still* raining, and just when she believed her luck couldn't get any worse, a gleaming black Rolls Royce swept past her into a puddle, which resembled a small reservoir, and all but drowned her in the backwash. Coming to a furious standstill as cold, muddy water dripped like sludge down the side of her fawn-coloured coat and turned her expensive matching shoes to a darker, grimier version of the concrete pavement, Sophie swore out loud. *Not just once—but three times, in quick violent succession*, each passionate utterance giving undisputed vent to her fury and indignation.

Narrowing her gaze, she saw to her surprise and satisfaction that the stately vehicle had slowed, then stopped at the side of the kerb. Not hesitating, she hurried towards it, her heart pumping with rage and her breath tight, her only concern that whoever was in there got a piece of her mind that they wouldn't soon forget. If Sophie had to arrive at her best friend's marriage ceremony looking as if she'd slept in a puddle beneath Waterloo bridge, then the occupant of that damned Rolls Royce was going to know that she prayed the same bad luck which had been visited on her today would dog the rest of *his* day.

She didn't for one moment doubt that the car's owner would be male. Only a thoughtless, insensitive *oaf* would deliberately drive through a puddle when he could clearly see her walking on the pavement beside it. But when she reached the car, a silver-haired chauffeur stepped out and looked immediately contrite.

'I'm so sorry, miss. We were in a hurry and I didn't see that confounded puddle until it was too late.'

'Well, *I'm* in a hurry, too, but you don't see me ruining someone else's day with my thoughtlessness, do you? You should have been more careful! Now what am I supposed to do?' Her freezing fingers curling stiffly around her umbrella handle, and the puddle that had soaked her shoes turning her feet to twin blocks of ice, Sophie had trouble keeping her teeth from chattering.

'Get back in the car, Louis. I don't have time for this. We're going to be late as it is.'

It was only at the sound of that coolly imperious voice that Sophie glanced into the passenger-seat window at the back of the car. Catching a glimpse of precision-cut wheat-blond hair and eyes as hard as flint, she felt a shiver run down her spine that had nothing to do with the cold or damp conditions she currently found herself in. The man's rapier-like instruction to his chauffeur, delivered as if he didn't give a damn what had happened to Sophie as long as he got to where *he* was going, made her blood boil.

'How dare you?' she shouted. 'I'm standing here soaked to the skin, my outfit ruined, because your stupid car happened to drive straight through a puddle the size of the River Thames, and all you can do is think about yourself and your own comfort! Well, I hope you have the worst day ever, I really do! You don't even have the guts to step out and face me, do you? Never mind apologise!'

'Miss…let me help you. I'm sure we could give you a lift to wherever you're going. We could—'

As the mortified chauffeur did his best to make amends for the ignorance of his boss, the passenger door suddenly opened and the man seated in the back of the car stepped out to gaze at Sophie with unconcealed disdain, as if she was an annoying drone buzzing around his dinner. He was very tall, and his height and breadth of shoulders alone, beneath his formal black coat, should have intimidated her. Green eyes, as crystal-clear and sharp as unflawed emeralds, studied her indignant features without so much as a flicker of emotion. *None.*

'What is it you want from me? You shouldn't have been walking so close to the kerb, and wearing such ridiculous shoes in this weather, too. You have only yourself to blame.'

Ridiculous shoes? Sparing a brief wounded glance down at her too-expensive open-toed cream high-heeled sandals, which she had splashed out on purely in deference to her friend's wedding, Sophie almost spluttered with rage.

'How dare you? What kind of footwear I put on my feet isn't your damned business remotely! I happen to be attending a special occasion... Not that that's any of your business, either. Am I supposed to have foreseen that some idiot would drive by and almost drown me? You have a bloody nerve, you know that?'

'I repeat…what do you want from me? Do you want me to reimburse you for the shoes or pay for your dry-cleaning? What? Tell me quickly so I can be on my way. I have already wasted valuable time standing here listening to you scream at me like a fishwife.'

He had some kind of accent, Sophie realised from his clipped speech. Dutch perhaps? But, more than that, she was reeling that he should dare to call her a fishwife just because she'd stood up for herself and hadn't let him simply get in his car and be driven away without making her feelings known.

Seeing him take out his wallet and extract some notes, she all but blanched. 'I don't want your damned money! Didn't it even occur to you that a simple gracious apology would do? I feel sorry for you…you know that? Driving around in your expensive car, hiding behind your tinted windows, acting like you run the world! Well, go on your way, Mister Whoever-you-are, and God forbid you're as late for your precious appointment as I'm clearly going to be for mine! But if you are—just remember the reason why, huh?'

About to turn on her unaccustomed high heel, Sophie was shocked into speechlessness by the blond giant's hand clamping suddenly around her more fragile wrist.

'If you don't want my money then perhaps a lift to wherever you are going would be more appropriate? Louis can drop me off at my own destination, then take you on to yours. Will that suffice?'

Knowing that it probably almost choked him to offer her a lift, and because her anger made her feel perverse, Sophie snatched her hand free and glared back at him with a distinct challenge in her large blue eyes. 'In the absence of an apology then a lift will have to suffice under the circumstances.' Biting her lip to prevent the more polite 'thank you' which threatened to follow her little speech, Sophie folded up her dripping umbrella and, at his instigation, preceded her reluctant host into the opulent hide-seated interior.

Feeling mutinous when her folded umbrella dripped muddy water all over the floor, she deliberately pursed her lips and stared out of the window while he settled himself as far away from her as possible at the other end of the seat. *Perhaps he thought he might catch something contagious?*

As the door slammed he said in a terse, reluctant voice, 'You may tell Louis where you are going when I get out.'

Not believing a reply to be necessary, Sophie glanced down at the time on her watch, then back out of the tinted glass window at the rainy London street. She couldn't help wondering if Diana was ever going to forgive her for turning up to her wedding late, and not only that, but looking like something the cat dragged in, too.

Minutes later, when the Rolls Royce purred to a halt outside a familiar-looking building, with wide curving steps leading up to its twin front doors, Sophie knitted her brows in confusion. She hadn't yet told Louis where she was going, so how come he'd just pulled up outside the same register office where Diana was getting married to Freddie? As she saw the blond Adonis beside her open the passenger door next to him, she frowned again. 'Wait a minute. This is where *I* need to be dropped off. I'm going to my friend's wedding.'

Cool green eyes assessed her confusion with the kind of haughtiness that was normally associated with royalty. It made Sophie bristle, as well as causing hot, indignant colour to flood into her cheeks.

'You are going to Diana Fitzwalter's wedding?' he demanded.

Now, how did he know that? And, more to the point, how did he know Diana? Sophie froze, as though she'd just lost her nerve on a tightrope walk, as the most obvious conclusion seeped slowly into her brain. *Was he going to Diana's wedding, too?*

'You know Diana?' she queried, her shock barely allowing her vocal chords to function.

'She is my personal assistant so, yes, obviously I know her.'

He was Dominic Van Straten? The billionaire property developer Diana worked for? The man who, according to her, found it hard to raise a smile even when the value of his stocks and shares had just shot through the roof and made him even richer? *But why on earth would Diana invite him to her wedding when Sophie and one of Freddie's friends were supposed to be the only witnesses because the couple wanted to keep the whole thing low-key?*

Even her confident, outgoing friend had admitted to Sophie that the man just plain intimidated her, and the only reason she stayed working for him was that her salary far exceeded most personal assistants', thereby allowing her a very comfortable lifestyle indeed.

Her legs feeling drained of strength, Sophie climbed out of the car behind him to finish speaking. 'Well, I'm Diana's friend…Sophie.'

Dominic didn't smile. Neither did he introduce himself. The light grooves bracketing his forbidding mouth stayed obstinately still, without the merest suggestion of a surprised or conciliatory gesture such as a rueful smile. *Well, what did she expect?* The man was about as warm as a frozen joint of beef straight out of the freezer.

Pushing her fingers through the short damp strands of her hair, Sophie glanced down at her watch, barely registering that they were five minutes late for the ceremony already because she was suddenly feeling drained of every bit of pleasure or hope of an enjoyable afternoon. She visibly shivered, and Dominic Van Straten's glacial glance flicked across her face with a flash of impatience before he turned and negotiated the wide concrete steps which led to the entrance of the building with an imposing long-legged stride.

In the vestibule they were greeted by a radiant-looking but anxious Diana, and her relieved and handsome fiancé, Freddie Carmichael.

'Sophie! Thank God! What on earth happened to you?' Diana's eyes widened in disbelief as she took in the dark greying stains on Sophie's fawn coat and the mud splashed up her cream hosiery and shoes.

Glancing briefly at her brooding and so far silent companion, Sophie shrugged. 'Car broke down and I had to walk. I'll tell you all about it later. Is it time to go in?'

'It is. Oh, God, I'm feeling nervous! How nice to see you, Dominic. I'm so glad you could come at such short notice. Trust Freddie's best pal to come down with flu! So good of you to act as stand-in. Shall we go in? I believe the registrar is waiting for us.'

All through the touching ceremony, it seemed to Sophie that Dominic expressed very little emotion of any kind. Not even a smile. His presence unnerved Sophie tremendously, she had to admit. When they both had to sign the marriage certificate as witnesses afterwards, he bent his blond head to the task as gravely as though he were signing someone's death certificate.

Diana had told Sophie that they were all going to lunch at the Park Lane Hilton where other friends were joining them, and Sophie found herself praying hard that Dominic wouldn't be accompanying them. Having to maintain a pretended civility towards a man she instinctively disliked would be like being forced to wear a tight Victorian corset that constricted her breathing for the afternoon.

She hadn't prayed hard enough. Half an hour later, holding a glass of crystal champagne in the foyer of the plush hotel to toast the bride and groom, her stained coat at last relegated to an obliging assistant in the cloakroom, and Dominic standing beside her, she gulped down her champagne too quickly and had an immediate coughing fit. The hand that clapped down on her back to try and ease her discomfort was surprisingly Dominic's.

'Here,' he said, 'let me take your glass until you compose yourself.'

'Oh, Soph! Are you all right, darling?' Diana appeared

at her other side, her hazel eyes full of concern. Smiling through the tears that had embarrassingly sprung to her eyes, Sophie nodded. Retrieving her glass from Dominic's large square hand, she wished the ground would open up and swallow her. She was having a pig of a day and no mistake! If anything else went wrong for her she vowed to herself she would simply go home, lock the door and devour a large box of chocolates, as recompense.

'I'm fine, thanks. Just went down the wrong way.'

'Oh, look who's just arrived! It's Katie and David. Will you excuse us for a moment, you two? We'll be right back.'

Before she could say anything, Sophie watched Diana glide away with her attentive new husband to greet the newcomers she had spotted in the foyer's entrance. Disconcertingly, she was left alone with Dominic. It was a little like being left alone in a sealed cage with a boa constrictor and a man-eating tiger, and probably twice as intimidating.

'The ceremony went well, don't you think?' Inwardly Sophie groaned as soon as the words were out of her mouth. *Now I sound like a character in an old English farce!* She thought with annoyance. It would probably be better if she stopped the pretence of civility right there and then, and simply ignored the hateful man. And she'd never forgive him if his taciturn and condescending manner ruined Diana's wedding day.

'Do you like weddings?' he asked her, surprisingly.

Seeing that there was still no hint of a smile or anything remotely friendly on his severe but handsome face, Sophie stared back at him defiantly. 'No. I hate them, as a matter of fact.'

'Why?'

Never having had to express her feelings about the subject before to a stranger, Sophie honestly wasn't sure how to explain her aversion. 'I find them…awkward. In my opinion Diana and Freddie did the right thing, keeping things simple. There's always some kind of horrible tension when families get together at these sorts of occasions, don't you think? Plus, you have to talk to people you'd rather not at the reception, and it's all very difficult.'

She reached the end of her sentence and clamped her mouth shut in horror at what she'd just said. Talk about putting her foot in it! But, to her consternation, Dominic didn't appear at all offended. Instead, a smile started to lurk around his lips, completely transforming that gravely serious face of his into something much more humane.

'I take it you are not married yourself, Sophie?'

'That's correct.' Her own manner now a little stiff, because she thought he must be thinking, *I'm not surprised*, she couldn't help flushing a little in embarrassment. She knew she wasn't exactly *plain* but she was hardly extraordinary, and the fact that he had already called her a 'fish wife' when she'd lost her temper with him didn't exactly help her case.

When he appeared not to be going to make any comment whatsoever, but simply studied her as though she were an interesting alien specimen that had flown in from Mars, Sophie honestly just wanted to go to the cloakroom, collect her ruined coat and flag down a taxi to take her home. She could pay for it when she got there. But, even though that was her strongest urge, she knew she would grit it out, for Diana. She wouldn't be the one fly in the ointment that spoiled her friend's wedding day. She would leave that particular little trick to Diana's very superior and aloof boss.

'You must let me reimburse you for your spoiled coat and shoes,' he said eventually, and Sophie squirmed with discomfort.

She didn't want to accept his money, or his sudden inclination to give it to her. She just wanted to get away from this horribly embarrassing situation that she found herself in as quickly as possible. Would Diana buy her story that she was up to her eyes in marking essays for her five-year-old pupils? *No. She didn't think so...*

'Look, Mr Van Straten. You don't like me, and I don't like you, so you don't have to reimburse me for anything, and we don't need to stand here making polite conversation when we'd both clearly prefer to be somewhere else! Why did you agree to be Diana's witness, by the way?'

If he was taken aback, either by her outburst or her question, again Dominic gave no sign. 'She asked me as a favour and I was happy to comply. That obviously surprises you, Sophie.'

It surprised the hell out of her that he even deigned to call her by her name, let alone pursue any further conversation with her after what had happened between them.

'Frankly, it does. You don't strike me as the kind of man who easily dispenses favours.'

'Oh? And so what kind of man *do* I strike you as, Sophie?'

Now she'd done it. The words *cold, remote, insensitive and superior* hovering on her tongue, she forged recklessly ahead instead with, 'Too self-contained and self-interested to notice others' needs if you want to know the truth.' Those words were probably worse.

Much worse, going by the glower that had suddenly replaced his previously more benign expression.

'You don't believe in mincing your words, do you? It does not surprise me that you are not married. A man likes a little verbal jousting, from time to time, Sophie, but he does not like a *shrew*.'

'I'm not a shrew!' It was true she had a temper, but it was only really roused by injustice of any kind. Like earlier, when Dominic's expensive regal car had splashed muddy water all over her nice clothes. Clothes that she was hard-pushed to afford on the ridiculously inadequate pay of a primary-school teacher.

Pursing her lips, Sophie held onto that temper by a thread, wishing that Diana would quickly come back and join them, to help alleviate the now increasingly uncomfortable tension between herself and this man.

'I'm not a shrew, but neither am I a woman who is scared to speak her mind. If it weren't for the kindness of your chauffeur, Mr Van Straten, you would have left me stranded and bedraggled by the roadside while you made your way to my best friend's wedding. Nothing you have said or done since makes me think that you have any redeeming qualities that I may have missed!'

'Even when I stopped you from choking?'

Sophie's blue eyes flew indignantly wide. 'You did not stop me from choking! My champagne went down the wrong way, that's all.'

'So I am too ''self-contained'' and ''self-interested'' to help someone in obvious distress? That is what you think?'

'Actions speak louder than words, so they say.'

'Then you need not worry that I will be joining you for lunch. I will not inflict my company upon you any longer.'

And, with that, Dominic abruptly turned his back on Sophie and left. With her heart throbbing beneath her ribs, she watched him cross the plushly carpeted foyer and go over to speak to Diana. Clearly seeing the surprise and dismay reflected on her friend's attractive face as he spoke to her, Sophie could have kicked herself for being the reason that Dominic was leaving. Obviously Diana wanted him there, or she wouldn't have asked him to stand in as a witness in the first place.

If only Sophie had been able to contain her temper! This day wasn't about her own comfort or discomfort. It was about Diana having one of the best days of her life. Now her best friend had thoughtlessly gone and ruined it!

Even though she disliked Dominic Van Straten with a passion, she still felt terribly guilty at driving him away. As soon she managed to get Diana on her own she confessed her feelings to her friend.

'I scared him off.'

She took another sip of champagne and screwed up her nose at a taste she wasn't sure she would ever become accustomed to. She needn't have worried. On a teacher's salary buying champagne was not exactly a dilemma.

'What do you mean, you scared him off?' Looking puzzled and beautiful, with her carefully styled blonde hair and her fitted ivory suit, Diana frowned. 'Nobody scares Dominic Van Straten away from anything! More like the other way round! He told me something important came up that he had to attend to. I thought that might happen. The man barely ever takes a break from his work. What a shame…especially as he's paying for all of this!'

'Your boss is paying for your wedding feast?' Now

Sophie was aghast. *You don't strike me as a man who dispenses favours easily...*she had said to him.

'He insisted. Including all the champagne we can drink. He's not the easiest man in the world to work for, but you can't fault his generosity.'

'Really?' Sophie's eyes slid guiltily away as she told herself it wasn't *her* fault if he was so easily offended. He *had*, after all, called her a *shrew*. Had he really expected her to forget that and carry on as normal? But this *was* Diana's special day, and she had clearly wanted her boss to be a part of the celebrations. *Why wouldn't she when he'd been decent enough to pay for everything?*

Honesty behoved Sophie to emphasise the truth more forcefully. 'Diana, listen, it really *is* my fault that Dominic left! We got off to a bad start. His car inadvertently splashed me with muddy water; that's why my coat was in such a state. Anyway, I'm afraid I lost my temper with him. Just now, before he left, things just went from bad to worse and I ended up insulting him rather badly.'

At the appalled look of disbelief on Diana's face, another surge of horrible guilt washed over Sophie. 'I didn't realise he'd paid for your wedding feast or I would have held onto my temper a bit better. I'm really sorry.'

'Oh, Sophie, what have you done?' Diana groaned, digging through her satin purse to find her mobile phone. 'I'll have to ring him and apologise. If I can persuade him to come back you've got to promise me you'll be on your best behaviour, or you and I won't stay friends for much longer! Do you understand?'

'Perhaps it would just be best if I left now?'

Knowing she was taking the coward's way out,

Sophie told herself that if Dominic conceded to return to the reception, and Diana enjoyed the rest of her day, then the fact that her best friend wouldn't be there would be worth it.

'Oh, no, you don't!' Grabbing her hand before she could take even one step towards the exit, Diana looked furious. 'You are going to stay here and face the music! If Dominic expects an apology from you then you are going to give it to him—do you hear me, Sophie? I am not having my wedding day ruined because you were rude to the one person I can't afford to let you be rude to!'

CHAPTER TWO

EATING humble pie had never been so painful. Later that evening, round the dining table, she deliberately avoided eye contact with Dominic.

After making her stammering apology, Sophie had lapsed into a painful and angry silence. The man hadn't even had the grace to accept her apology like a gentleman. Instead, he'd arrogantly replied, 'I will accept your apology, Sophie…for Diana's sake,' then continued to talk to Freddie—Diana's husband—as though Sophie no longer existed.

Sophie had never felt more belittled or disgruntled in all her life. He had got the upper hand again, and it was clear he was going to make Sophie suffer as a consequence. Right then, as she studied his handsome, hard-jawed profile, she honestly *despised* the man. She was glad for Diana's sake that he had relented and returned to the reception, but she almost would have preferred ex-communication from Diana's friendship than endure the vehement discomfort that she was currently having to endure.

When the guests moved into the bar area, where a tuxedo-attired pianist was entertaining the hotel residents with some gentle jazz, Sophie wondered how long in all conscience she should stay, before telling Diana she was leaving? Standing alone as she sipped the glass of wine she had brought with her from the table, Sophie glanced up startled as she suddenly found herself face to face with Dominic.

For a long moment he just stared at her, saying nothing. Her spine prickling with resentment, Sophie remembered that she had promised Diana not to let her temper run away with her again. At least as far as *this* man was concerned. *But, God, it was hard!* Swallowing razorblades would surely be easier?

'Having a nice time?' she asked, then coloured as she realised he could easily interpret such a remark as facetious.

'I can tell you are not happy that I came back, Sophie.' One corner of his mouth curled back into his smooth cheek. She focused her gaze on the two black buttons on his jacket instead of being persuaded to look into his eyes, unreasonably annoyed that his eyes should be so disagreeably hypnotic and so unrelentingly *green*.

'Whatever gave you that idea?'

Now she *did* sound facetious. Dammit! It was nigh on impossible to be agreeable to this man when he clearly thought himself so much better than everyone else. Stealing a look over Dominic's broad shoulder, in its perfectly tailored jacket, Sophie caught a pointed glimpse of Diana's definitely raised eyebrow. It was as if she were silently saying to Sophie, *Remember your promise? Don't go ruining anything else!*

Sophie swallowed hard, and somehow managed to persuade her mostly uncooperative lips into a smile up at Dominic.

For a moment he registered surprise. Then he glanced round, saw that she'd been looking at Diana, and turned back with a slight disapproving tilt of his jaw. *She had to be the most difficult and argumentative woman he had ever come across,* Dominic thought. But she had pretty eyes, and a torturously sexy mouth, and even though her ill manners exasperated him she stirred a surprising heat inside him that he couldn't deny. In fact, as he took another careful sip of his wine Dominic let that heat sizzle a little in sudden concentrated anticipation that he might turn his verbal conflagration with Sophie into a conflagration of a very *different* but much more pleasurable sort. If she wasn't passive by nature, there was no way that the woman would be passive in bed.

Quite unexpectedly, the thought became urgent and goal-orientated, until Dominic found he could think of nothing he'd like more than getting Sophie between the sheets and indulging in the kind of sexual sparring that excited him most. Before the night was through, he vowed to have her purring rather than wanting to scratch his eyes out!

'Your glass is almost empty, I see. How about some more champagne?'

Before Sophie could even register his intention, Dominic had deftly removed her glass from her hand and, glancing round him, signalled a nearby waiter to give him her glass and an order for more drinks. When he turned back to Sophie, levelling his disturbing gaze on her eyes and then her mouth, as if he would devour her down to her very bones, her senses were suddenly besieged by a wave of desire so ignitable that for a moment she couldn't think, let alone form words.

Rocked to the very toes of her expensive cream sandals, she wondered what the hell was wrong with her? *She disliked this smug, arrogant man intensely, never mind desired him! She must have had too much champagne and wine. That was the only logical conclusion she could come to right then.* She had better slow things right down before she committed one more act of utter and complete folly, and so thoroughly made a fool of herself that she wouldn't be able to live with herself again.

'I really don't think I ought to have any more alcohol,' she confessed, aghast at the fact that her composure had been thrown so off kilter by his too-intimate cynosure. 'I'm not really used to drinking.'

'If not drinking, then surely you must have other vices, Sophie? I wonder what they might be?'

Her attention trapped indisputably by the suggestive honeyed tones of his mesmerising voice, Sophie couldn't look away. She wanted to make some clever or cutting little quip, to put a dent in his too-confident leer, but her throat and her thoughts seemed to dry up at the same time, and nothing sprang helpfully to mind.

'Sophie? Are you all right?'

He touched her; laid his hand on her bare arm and gave it a definite *squeeze*. There was no question in Sophie's mind that he had somehow *branded* her. Now her senses were jumping around all over the place in utter and wild confusion, and the place where he had lain his fingers felt as if it were on fire. *Why was it that when she looked into that intimidatingly handsome face of his she knew she hated him? Yet when he had touched her just now she had almost swayed with the sheer intoxicating pleasure of it?* Today was turning out to be one of the most bizarre days in recent memory that was for sure!

'I'm fine. I was just—I just felt a little cold…that's all.'

'Cold?' A surprised eyebrow lifted towards Dominic's crown of blond hair, accompanied by a very wry and disbelieving smile. The room was almost too hot. And he could plainly see that Sophie's cheeks were burning. In that very moment Dominic knew without a doubt she was having trouble diverting her attraction towards him. Just as he was having trouble doing the same thing with her. *In his mind there was only one solution to their mutual problem.*

'How were you planning on getting home this evening?' he asked, his voice deceptively casual as his eyes met the startled blue of her anxious gaze.

'Home?' *Good God! Now she had completely lost the ability to converse at all. She'd turned into a monosyllabic idiot!* Determinedly Sophie made herself focus. Was he going to offer her a lift? she speculated.

'Oh, I'll probably cadge a lift off one of Diana's friends, or get a taxi.'

'I was wondering…as an alternative…' Dominic moved closer, and his fingers found their way beneath Sophie's chin and lifted it up a little. Her bones were so delicate and fine that she felt the strong imprint of his fingers acutely. Inside, her heart felt as if it was just about to go into cardiac arrest, and she waited for him to finish speaking all thoughts of Diana, Freddie, and their friends vanished as if they no longer existed. The only two people left in the room were herself and Dominic. '…whether you might like to stay the night in the hotel, with me?'

'Sta—stay the night?' she repeated, once more appalled at how this man could affect her so acutely with just one smooth, confident glance. *Was he serious?* The thought that he might be stringing her along, to pay her back for insulting him earlier, struck a very loud alarm bell in Sophie's head. He had turned on the charm, reeled her in, and now he was going to dump her in an even bigger metaphorical puddle than the real one that had drenched her earlier!

She circled her fingers around his wrist and threw his hand away. 'You must think me completely stupid if you think I'm going to fall for that kind of obvious little ruse! I'm on to you, Mr Van Straten! I know all you're trying to do is pay me back because I spoke my mind earlier, and didn't bow and scrape like you usually expect people to do in your exalted company!'

Dominic couldn't help but laugh. It simply hadn't occurred to him that she might think his invitation to bed was some kind of game he was playing to repay her for insulting him! She was a defensive little creature, that was for sure. He would have to convince her he meant no offence at all—*quite the opposite in fact.*

'You have it all wrong Sophie. There was no affront intended. Nor do I expect you to ''bow and scrape'' in my company. I *do*, however, desire very much that you share my bed tonight. I am perfectly serious about this, and there is no trick up my sleeve with which I am trying to hoodwink you. Understand?' He saw the confusion in her eyes, the slight flush that rushed into her cheeks, and the way her hands nervously went to her hair. Feeling his desire grow, Dominic slid his hand around the curve of her cheek and jaw, and gently stroked the skin that was as beguiling to the touch as the most opulent velvet.

'*Understand?*' he repeated more softly.

Dominic had taken off Sophie's shoes. Sitting on the bed, with its rich claret-coloured satin counterpane, her hands intertwined in her lap, it was hard for her to stop trembling like a shivering kitten that had been left out in the rain as he knelt before her. *She wanted him to kiss her. Wanted it so badly that her very bones ached with longing.* Instead, she watched entranced as he divested himself of his jacket and tie, opened some buttons on his shirt and—with his gaze fixed firmly on hers—slid his palms up the outside of her stockinged thighs.

The blue silk of her dress rippled like a gentle flowing stream as he edged it further and further up her legs. She was wearing a cream-coloured suspender belt with little embossed daisies on it to hold up her matching cream hosiery, and Sophie wondered what Dominic would think of her undoubtedly sexy underwear? *Would he imagine she'd worn it just in case she got lucky?* Because this was so far from the truth, and she was unable to keep her pained thoughts to herself, she inadvertently released a groan. Dominic smiled at her with a slow, engagingly sexy smile of acknowledgement, and a spark of molten heat burned back at her from his darkened green eyes as he flipped open the fastenings that held her stockings up and slowly…very slowly…peeled them down her bare legs.

Excitement and all-consuming need thrummed commandingly through Dominic's blood. Seducing a beautiful woman was one of life's most exquisite pleasures, after all, and he knew the seductive arts as well as he knew how to make a million dollars without exerting himself. The skill had become innate. Knowing how to take things slowly—how to drive a woman's passion to such a crescendo that she would beg him to take her, to ease her agony—he was perfectly acquainted with bestowing sensual delectation.

But, right now Dominic was the one who was in desperate need of this woman's touch. He needed it—no, *craved* it, as if he would lose his mind if he didn't have it soon. With her eyes blinking back at him like a startled owl's, Dominic registered her tension—her *excitement* and, linking his fingers expertly around the sides of the scant silk panties she was wearing, he gave them a gentle tug downwards. Quickly removing them, he settled his body nearer hers on the bed, whilst still kneeling on the carpet, and this time slid his palms up the insides of her trembling legs.

Hearing her deeply in-drawn breath, Dominic caressed the fine dark curls at her apex, then worked his fingers inside her. At the sensation of hot moist heat, that drenched him, he could not prevent his own gasp of violent pleasure.

Oh, God, yes! More please more! Don't stop. Sophie's thoughts were desperate and wild as Dominic worked his magic, making her climax almost before she even knew that was her destination. Feeling heat saturate her, and her aroused nipples rub acutely sensitively against the flimsy material of her bra inside her dress, she expelled her breath in soft urgent gasps of deliciously lustful pleasure. Tipping back her head, she shut her eyes in ecstasy as erotic waves rippled powerfully through her, one after the other.

She'd never known release like it. Such mind-spinning pleasure had only been pure fantasy for Sophie up until now.

Opening her eyes again, she saw that Dominic had discarded his shirt and was doing the same to his trousers. Her gaze devoured him greedily. *His body was amazing.* Broad, beautifully muscled shoulders and chest, an iron-hard stomach tapering down to lean, tight hips, a sprinkling of fine blond hairs disappearing tantalisingly down into his black silk boxers. Sophie inadvertently dampened her lips with her tongue.

Dominic honed in on the unknowingly erotic gesture with such a possessive, hungry glance that she almost climaxed again, right there and then. Then, rising over her on the bed, he tipped up her chin and brought his lips down hard and hot upon hers. His tongue was a seductive instrument of velvet torture as he played with and teased Sophie's mouth, nipping and stroking her tender flesh with ruthless prowess.

His expertise took kissing to a whole new dimension. The taste of him was the most destroyingly addictive nectar her lips had ever experienced, and she wasn't ashamed to silently admit she wanted more. Reaching for the hem of her silk dress, he lifted it over Sophie's head in one quick, fluid movement, then undid her lacy cream bra in the same expert fashion.

'You are perfect,' he breathed in wonder, as his hand cupped the soft swell of one full pink-tipped breast and then the other.

'Not as perfect as you,' Sophie couldn't help replying, putting her hand out to touch his bare, flat stomach. Her fingers touched velvet steel, and she sucked in a deep breath in purely sensual satisfaction.

'Yes,' Dominic agreed, his voice a silken rasp, 'touch me, Sophie. I *want* you to touch me.'

His command opened the floodgates of need inside her. Greedily she slid her hand down, past his perfect navel, past the springy clutch of fine blond hairs, and grasped his hard, hot erection. *He felt like satin.* As her fingers curled around him Dominic groaned, then bent his head and kissed Sophie again, drinking from her moist, plundered lips with increasing urgency and ardour. She offered no protest when he guided her firmly down onto the bed and positioned his strong, muscular thighs either side of her.

Just before she lost the power to think of anything else but the intense gratification to come, Sophie knew she ought to tell Dominic that she was on the Pill. She took it more to help regulate her periods than for more obvious reasons, but even as she opened her mouth to speak she saw him reach into the trousers he had discarded and withdraw a small blue packet.

As he slipped off his boxers and sheathed himself in the protection she saw for herself how generously endowed he was, and her mouth went dry as chalk. She forgot the fact that they were supposed to be enemies, that they didn't have a single thing in common between them except this: *this wild, inexplicable sexual attraction that had flared up between them hotly and unexpectedly and compelled them to go to bed together.* And when Dominic brought his mouth down upon her breasts, attending to each one in turn with hot, demanding caresses, urging her towards the most intense delectation she had ever known, Sophie decided not to fight her conscience at all, but simply just to enjoy the experience instead.

Didn't her friends do that all the time? Not the ones who were looking for Mr Right, but the others, who believed it was a woman's right to take sexual pleasure wherever she could find it and suffer no guilt.

'Are you ready for me, Sophie?' Dominic whispered against her ear, as he slid his hard, fit body along hers. 'Are you going to let me inside now?'

Was that husky little whimper really hers? Was that soft, needy voice really the same vehemently strident one that had levelled all those insults at him just a few short hours ago? As he urged her slender thighs apart, and pushed slowly but firmly inside her, Sophie ran her hands down Dominic's back, pressing her fingernails into his toned muscled flesh with increasing need as he thrust deeply inside her.

'That's it, my little cat... Let me feel your pretty little claws.'

Dominic had always been blessed with a healthy libido, but even *he* had not experienced sexual need so intensely passionate as this. His lips became intimately acquainted with every inch of her flesh in a hungry search to sate himself with her body. *Even her sweat tasted sweet to his beguiled mouth.*

Holding back his own desperate compulsion to reach a climax, Dominic thrust into Sophie again and again, until she came undone in his arms. As she quivered and moaned, and slid her hands down the now slippery wetness of his back, he succumbed to a wave of ecstasy so powerful and glorious that he was left breathless and stunned in its aftermath. Before he rolled away from her, Dominic stared down into Sophie's lovely blue eyes and smiled at her with the most deeply satisfied smile he had ever bestowed on a lover before.

'You have nothing to say to me now my, little cat?' he taunted gently, green eyes brimming with amusement and fierce, fierce pleasure.

Staring up into the hard, lean contours of his mesmerising face, her body already needing him again, and throbbing with unashamed anticipation, Sophie sighed softly up at him.

'Sometimes words aren't necessary…don't you think?' she whispered, her glance already sliding away from his, in case she exposed herself too deeply to his hot, examining gaze…

About to race out of the door because she was late, Sophie was delayed by the appearance of a courier with a large package that she had to sign for. Puzzled by what the contents could possibly be, she nonetheless signed the delivery note quickly, left the box on the table just inside the front door, and dashed down the road to catch the bus that would take her to the primary school where she taught.

The local garage did not hold out much hope for her beloved car, so she had no choice other than to use public transport to get to work. The young mechanic who had looked over it for her had shaken his head and cheerfully told Sophie that it didn't have much value other than scrap. His blasé conclusion pained her deeply. Any repairs she might instruct them to undertake would apparently cost her almost twice that of the value of the car itself. Her heart sinking, she'd agreed to let them tow it away, and resigned herself to getting used to either Shanks's pony or the unreliable delights of the local transportation system. She certainly wasn't in the market for a new car—second-hand or otherwise.

Diana's wedding and the whole difficult day on Friday—culminating in the most surprising event of all, when she and Dominic had ended up in bed together—he'd vowed not to think about too much.

How had she allowed herself to behave like such an unbelievable little hussy? Even now she couldn't quite believe she had succumbed so easily to the ruthless charm of Diana's handsome boss. Coming to her senses in the early hours of Saturday morning, she had been careful not to wake him in the bed beside her, and instead had paid a brief visit to the bathroom, dressed quickly, then left the hotel without so much as saying goodbye to him. *What was the point?* In the harsh, cold light of morning she knew they'd both only regret their passionate fling.

No…Sophie had *definitely* done the right thing where Dominic Van Straten was concerned. She'd saved them both the embarrassment of confronting each other again.

No doubt he'd been nothing but relieved when he'd woken to find her gone.

Now, on Monday morning, Sophie found that she actually welcomed the chattering voices of her class of sixteen lively five-year-olds in preference to ever enduring such an uncomfortable occasion as Diana's wedding ever again. Whenever her unguarded mind recalled Dominic's intoxicating presence, her stomach reacted with an anxious, confused flip, and she was surprised yet again how one beguiling yet infuriating stranger could make her respond with such violent emotion.

She'd never had a one-night stand in her life before, and to have one with her best friend's boss, and on her wedding day, too, was probably the most uncharacteristic and reckless thing she'd ever done.

It was a good job Diana and Freddie had left before they'd found out that Sophie had agreed to spend the night with Dominic, or else she'd never have gone through with it in the first place. But even as she tried to reassure herself she would not willingly have embarrassed her friend—she knew she could not have resisted Dominic's invitation that night—not when his eyes had undressed her and openly made love to her even before they had reached the hotel room!

'Finish the story, Miss!'

'What?' Snapping out of yet another recollection of the Dutch billionaire who seemed to be dominating her thoughts with alarming regularity that morning, Sophie flushed guiltily, adjusted the illustrated book in her lap, and smiled warmly down at the group of children gathered round her seat on the floor. 'Where were we?'

'The big bad wolf was just about to gobble up the grandmother!' a little girl with blonde bobbed hair offered enthusiastically.

Sophie didn't miss the irony that she should be reading the story of Little Red Riding Hood and the Big Bad Wolf when her mind was preoccupied with thinking about Dominic…

The first thing she saw when she came through the door that evening was the package. Carrying it into the living room, Sophie shucked off the navy-blue duffel coat she'd been wearing over her skirt and sweater and laid the box down on the coffee table to examine the contents. There was a label on the back that announced the name of a well-known and expensive store in Knightsbridge, and Sophie frowned as she looked at it, wondering who on earth would be sending her anything from such an exclusive shop.

She came from an honest, hard-working, working-class family, and certainly her mum or dad or even her brother Phillip wouldn't dream of sending her expensive presents totally out of the blue..and neither would Sophie want them to. As she opened the box and stared down at the contents she sucked in her breath in astonishment.

It was a coat…the same fawn colour as her own, but made from cashmere, with a luxurious cream silk lining. Lifting it out to examine it more closely, Sophie saw to her amazement that it was the perfect size and length for her shape and height. Laying it down carefully on her threadbare burgundy couch, she searched around in the elegant tissue paper for a note of some kind, even though by now she had a pretty good idea who had sent it.

By the time she'd located the small gold-embossed business card, with 'Dominic' scrawled across one side in an impressive flourish, her heart was just about ready to burst out of her chest. Sophie couldn't remember telling him her address, but at some point in the evening she guessed she must have. After they'd made love they'd had more champagne brought to the room, and Sophie had been uncharacteristically giggly and talkative because of it.

She groaned out loud as she remembered. *But why was Dominic sending her such an expensive coat when all they'd had was a one-night stand?* Was it meant to be some kind of veiled insult or a reproach to make Sophie feel cheap? Was that it? He'd said he'd meant no affront when he'd asked her to go to bed with him, *but what if he'd lied?* Her heart plummeted like a stone. *What if he was teaching her a lesson? A horrible and despicable one, but a lesson in his eyes all the same?*

He might have been an expert lover, and he might have made her blood zing, but it was still a fact that Dominic Van Straten was completely out of Sophie's sphere. *What would demonstrate that fact more completely than sending the 'poor little working class girl' an expensive coat in payment for her 'services' at the hotel the other night?* Just because he'd made love to her, it didn't mean that he wasn't still arrogant, and even possibly cruel.

Her first instinct was to fold the coat back into its expensive packaging and mail it right back to him, and even as the thought came into her mind Sophie found herself arranging the coat back into the box in a fever of indignation and rage. Reading the card again, she looked for an address and found it. Surprisingly, it wasn't his office address, but his home one: Mayfair, London. Where else would a property developer billionaire live?

Seeing that there was a telephone number included beneath the address, Sophie went to the telephone in the hallway with thumping heart. If he thought she'd given him a piece of her mind on Friday, he'd better watch out! What did he think she was? Some kind of loose woman who'd gladly accept his no-doubt insulting gift of an expensive coat without a murmur? If he thought that, then he had a very big shock in store!

'Mr Van Straten's residence,' announced a cultured male voice at the other end of the line.

'I'd like to speak to Mr Van Straten,' Sophie announced as a flood of adrenaline shot through her system and almost made her sway. He was probably conveniently out.. or if he was at home no doubt he would instruct his butler, or whoever it was that had answered the phone, to tell her he wasn't available as soon as he knew it was Sophie.

'Whom shall I say is calling?' the voice at the other end came back.

Licking her suddenly dry lips, Sophie stared blankly at the picture on the wall, a well-known Degas print of ballerinas at the barre, going through their exercises. Shocked that he was actually at home, she told herself to keep her head and not give way to shrillness of any kind when she told him what he could do with his expensive gift. He'd already accused her of being a 'shrew' and a 'fishwife,' and if he insulted her with any such labels one more time, he'd rue the day!

'Sophie Dalton.'

She'd been about to explain that she was a friend of his assistant, Diana, then had thought, How ridiculous! If Dominic didn't condescend to remember her after what had occurred between them on Friday night then he was even more arrogant and despicable than she'd thought, and therefore even less deserving of any respect.

'Sophie. What a pleasant surprise!'

His voice shocked her into silence. It was disconcertingly familiar, and much too compelling to ever be taken lightly. On the telephone, his tone was sexier and much more troubling to her peace of mind than it had a right to be. It made her remember him asking seductively, *'Are you ready for me Sophie?'* Hot embarrassed colour surged into her face at the recollection.

'I wish I could say I felt the same, Dominic, but I can't. About the coat you sent me, I—'

'I trust it's the right size? I confess I had to guess your measurements, but then I do pride myself on being uncannily accurate when it comes to such things.'

He meant women...and their bodies. Was she just one of *many* female bodies he had undressed? Furious and hurt at the same time, she had to take a moment to compose herself. 'Whether it's the right size or not doesn't concern me! You had no right to send it to me in the first place. Especially when I know you are only trying to insult me!'

'Insult you?' Dominic said something beneath his breath that she didn't quite catch, and Sophie smoothed her hand down over her hip and reminded herself to keep her temper.

'Yes, insult me! Why else would you send it? You were making some sleazy point, no doubt, to thank me for services rendered. Well, you know what you can do with your expensive cashmere, don't you? I'll be mailing the coat straight back to you tomorrow! Just as soon as I can get to the Post Office.'

'My chauffeur accidentally splashed your coat with cold muddy water, Sophie...remember? I was merely trying to make amends by sending you a new one.

Anything else is completely a figment of your over-sensitive imagination.'

'Why make amends now, when you seemed not to care one jot about my situation on Friday, at Diana's wedding? Just because I was foolish enough to sleep with you, Dominic, it doesn't mean I'm a complete fool! I don't want your expensive gifts, do you hear? Whatever your reasons for sending me the coat, I have no intention of accepting it, or being beholden to you in any way.'

Dominic didn't know many women who would be insulted by the gift of a very expensive coat from one of the country's top exclusive stores. No—he had to re-phrase that. He knew for a fact that there were *no* women of his acquaintance that would have reacted in such an unexpected way. The women in his life had always adored the fact that he had the wealth and taste to pur-chase such expensive gifts for them—even the ones who came from money themselves.

Again, in spite of his irritation with Sophie for think-ing he was trying to insult her, Dominic sensed the blood heat in his veins as though it were being pursued by a fire. The memory of flashing blue eyes the colour of cornflowers started an ache inside him that suddenly made moving too quickly a hazard. He knew she was passionate and principled…if misguided…and she had been a totally responsive and highly provocative lover. He had not arranged for the coat to be sent as an insult in any way. He had certainly not sent it as *payment* for sexual services. He had most *definitely* sent it as a reason to speak to Sophie again.

When he'd woken up on Saturday morning and found her gone he'd barely been able to believe it. No woman had left him that way before…*ever*! Initially irked, he'd told himself she must have had some appointment to rush off to. Why else would she not have waited at least to say good morning? When he'd calmed down, and reflected on the sensational sex they'd enjoyed the night before, Dominic had also known that Sophie hadn't left because they hadn't hit it off together. Whatever her reasons for leaving, one thing he hadn't doubted was that she would naturally want to see him again. *Why wouldn't she?* When she rang him to thank him for the coat, as he'd fully expected her to do, Dominic had been planning on inviting her out for dinner. *The sooner the better, as far as he was concerned, because he hadn't been able to get the woman out of his mind.* Which was why he had included a card with his home address and telephone number on.

'How does accepting my gift make you beholden to me?' *If only it did*, Dominic thought, in frustration. It had been a long while since a woman had commanded his attention in such an emphatic way. He probably just needed to go to bed with her a few more times, to get her out of his system, he acknowledged with typical male frankness. *If she gave him the chance...*

'It just does.'

Suddenly tired of verbal sparring, and with her growling stomach letting her know that she hadn't eaten a thing since lunchtime, Sophie had it in her mind to end their fruitless conversation there and then. Tomorrow she would send Dominic the coat back, and that would be that. Her time and her thoughts would surely be better served this evening in working out how she was going to afford another car to get to school in. She couldn't rely on the vagaries of public transport. The head of the primary school in which she worked was a real stickler for punctuality, and Sophie knew it. It wouldn't do to

get on the wrong side of him and blot her so far un-
blemished record.

'Anyway,' she added, once more examining the print
of the pretty ballerinas on the wall, 'I'll have to say
goodnight. I've just got in from work, I'm tired and hungry, and I've got schoolwork to arrange for tomorrow.'

'Schoolwork?'

'I'm a teacher.'

'Diana didn't mention it.'

Not believing even for a second that a man so high
up in the echelons of wealth and personal achievement
would deign to discuss something as mundane as his
assistant's friends, with her, Sophie sighed. 'Why should
she? Goodbye, Dominic.'

'Why did you rush off like that on Saturday morning?'

Sophie wished he would leave the subject of Saturday
morning *and specifically Friday night* alone. She felt bad
enough about succumbing to her baser instincts so recklessly, *and* with the most unsuitable man she could
imagine!

'You may find this hard to believe, Dominic, but I'm
not the kind of woman who usually goes in for one-
night stands. In fact, this was the first…and I hope the
last one ever. It was an emotional day for me, and I—
my judgement wasn't at its best. You can rest assured I
won't be bothering you again in any way.'

*Dominic doubted that. Just thinking about the way she
had curled her slender legs around his back and driven
her nails into his flesh, in the throes of passion made
him almost too hot and bothered for words!* And what
did she mean her judgement hadn't been at its best? Was
she suggesting that making love with him had been a
mistake? Now, that *did* hit at the heart of his pride.

'If you won't accept the coat, why don't you bring it

to my house instead of mailing it?' Dominic suggested
smoothly, his calm tone belying the myriad of feelings
flooding through him.

Her senses hijacked by surprise and shock, Sophie bit
down on her lip. 'Bring it to your house?' she repeated,
not sure that she'd heard him correctly.

'Tomorrow—after work. You have the address on my
card?'

'Why are you doing this, Dominic?'

'I would like to talk to you about Diana,' he replied.

'Diana?' Drawing her brows together in confusion,
Sophie glanced down at the floor. Some of the maroon
carpet tiles were curling at the edges and needed replacing. A sudden wave of irritation and uncharacteristic de-
spondency briefly descended. She totally loved her job—
teaching for Sophie was a vocation—but she wished not
for the first time that it paid better and allowed her to
maintain a slightly better standard of living.

'I want to buy her a wedding present…something special. I thought perhaps you could advise me.'

Taken aback, Sophie really didn't know what to say.

'Well?' Dominic prompted into the heavy silence that
ensued.

'Aren't you supposed to buy a present in time for the
actual event?'

'I was away in Singapore on a business trip the week
leading up to her wedding, so I did not get a chance to
arrange a suitable gift for her.'

But he'd paid for her wedding breakfast just the same,
Sophie reluctantly recalled. Diana had said he was generous. She immediately discarded the thought with irritation.

'I'm sure you don't need me to advise you what to
buy Diana.' She shrugged, wondering why he should

suggest such a surprising thing when she had already professed herself insulted by his gift of the coat. *She would have thought he'd be glad not to get himself further entangled with Diana's 'unsuitable' friend.*

'You are her close friend. You know her tastes, her preferences. That information could help me a lot in choosing a gift she would really like.' His voice was almost hypnotically persuasive, and Sophie couldn't believe she was actually hesitating over her natural instinct to refuse.

She'd told herself that Friday night had probably meant nothing very much to a man like Dominic, other than sexual gratification with an available, attractive woman. She'd told herself she could handle it, despite feeling somehow 'used' when she received that beautiful coat as a gift. Now her feelings were all mixed up, and even more confused.

'Isn't there anyone else you could ask?' Even as she uttered the question Sophie knew she was clutching at straws. Dammit! She was nervous about going to Dominic's house. Who wouldn't be? It wasn't every day that an ordinary girl like her got invited to a billionaire's home! *Especially one she'd had a hot one-night stand with!* She'd be nervous even if they *hadn't* slept together.

'Is it too much to ask that you might do this for your friend?' Deftly and without remorse, Dominic slid home his advantage.

'No. No, of course not. I'll come, then. What time?'

'I will send Louis to collect you at about eight o'clock. I will see you then, Sophie.'

CHAPTER THREE

DETERMINEDLY clutching the large box containing the coat she was returning, Sophie glanced nervously through the stained glass panels on the swish and elegant Regency front door, and willed the butterflies in her stomach to cease their incessant fluttering just for a moment.

She wasn't looking forward to seeing Dominic Van Straten again one little bit. Right now she felt as if she'd voluntarily agreed to step up to the guillotine and have her head separated from her body. *That* was how much she hated the idea of even being here—no matter how beautiful or imposing the house in front of her, or how exclusive the address, or the fact that she'd just been transported there in a chauffeur-driven car.

Sophie could find no pleasure in any of it. She just wanted to return the damn coat and get out of there as fast as her legs could carry her. But when the door opened graciously before her eyes, and an elderly man dressed in a dark suit with neatly combed grey hair stood before her with a smile that was inordinately polite, she forced herself to speak and go forward.

'Hello. I'm Sophie Dalton. I have—I have an appointment with Mr Van Straten.'

'Of course. Please come in, Miss Dalton. Mr Van Straten is waiting for you in the drawing room. Shall I take your coat?'

Quickly unbuttoning it, while the man briefly held her package for her, Sophie wished she could have refused.

But it seemed churlish and ignorant to be deliberately difficult with a man she'd never even met before, so she handed it to him and gratefully took back the package. Trying not to goggle at the magnificent entrance hall, with its elegant air of grace and opulence and its fine, grey-veined white marble floor, Sophie obediently allowed him to lead her to Dominic. After announcing her arrival at the entrance to the room, the manservant discreetly withdrew, and closed the doors behind her.

It didn't take her long to locate the man she'd come to see. He was standing by the white marble fireplace, a drink in his hand, his lips slightly curving in a smile that appeared without question to be self-satisfied and slightly smug. What was he thinking? Was he gloating that he'd been able to persuade her to do as he'd asked?

Sophie almost retreated back the way she'd come. Although the room was gracious and elegant in the extreme, the most intimidating, magnetic element in it was Dominic himself. He was the pivot around which all that exceptionally good taste revolved. Even at the not inconsiderable distance between them she couldn't fail to see that it was his very presence that marked their surroundings more than anything else.

As his emerald eyes examined her with cool detachment and, yes...perhaps arrogance, Sophie told herself she must have lost her mind to have come here. Wasn't it enough that she'd shamed herself by sleeping with him the first day they had met? Was she really so eager to entertain even more embarrassment?

Feeling her lip quiver slightly with nerves, Sophie clamped down her teeth to quell it. 'I brought the coat...like I—like I said I would,' she announced, desperately trying to rescue her rapidly dwindling confidence.

'So I see,' he said.

An awkward silence descended. Sophie had just about decided to make her excuses and leave when Dominic put his glass down on the mantelpiece, moved away from the fireplace, and gestured towards the long white couch behind her. 'Why don't you sit down? We can discuss the coat later.'

'There's nothing to discuss. I don't want it, so I'm returning it.'

Defiant, and determined not to let him get the better of her in any way, Sophie placed the box down on the glass table in front of her, and did not shy away from the definite irritation in his gaze that he directed back.

'Nevertheless…I still think you should sit down. What can I get you to drink?'

She didn't want a drink, and she didn't want to sit down. All Sophie really wanted to do was leave. But, quelling her almost overwhelming desire to escape, she forced herself to sit down on the couch, and folded her hands neatly in front of her on her lap. Glancing around the beautiful room, with its exquisite antique furniture and imposing art on the walls, she was suddenly seized with uncharacteristic self-consciousness.

She hadn't dressed up in any way, shape or form for this little interview with Dominic. She'd kept on what she'd worn to school that morning: a red V-necked wool sweater, and a black calf-length skirt with matching low-heeled boots. And she'd deliberately not fussed with her usual minimal make-up either. She hadn't even reapplied her lipstick. There was no way that she was going to make Dominic imagine for one moment that she'd make any sort of effort with her appearance for his benefit. Sophie wasn't interested in what the man thought about what she looked like, or even if he thought about it at all. The sooner they discussed what they had to discuss the sooner she could be out of there, and heading home again.

'I'm fine,' she replied coolly. 'I had a cup of coffee before your chauffeur arrived to pick me up.'

'I didn't mean coffee. Will you have a Scotch or a brandy? It's cold outside. It will help warm you up.'

Even as he said the words, Dominic doubted very much whether any amount of alcohol could effect a thaw in Little Miss Frigid sitting over there on his couch. He hadn't expected this coldness after what had transpired between them on Friday night, and the fact that she clearly took no pleasure in either his company or his beautiful house seriously bothered him. Whatever people said about him, when he invited them into his home he wanted them to feel welcome.

Seeing her again, Dominic realised how much he'd been anticipating her visit. With her vivid blue eyes and her short, dark hair curling becomingly round her small ears, she was even prettier than he'd remembered—despite her frostiness towards him. And he couldn't deny the warm little charge of electricity that was surging through him just by being in the same room with her. He'd thought he'd let his feverish imagination run away with him where Sophie's appeal was concerned, but now he saw that he hadn't. He just couldn't understand this wild desire he was harbouring for a woman who was now displaying all the signs of complete uninterest and none of the passionate attraction she'd demonstrated on Friday. It certainly pricked his pride.

'I'd rather not, thank you. You said you wanted to talk about a wedding gift for Diana?'

Reaching into the discreet side pocket in her skirt, Sophie withdrew a folded piece of paper and, getting to her feet, handed it to Dominic. 'I've scribbled down some ideas that might help. Of course, not knowing what kind of budget you had in mind, my suggestions might be somewhat limited.'

A smile touching his lips at the mere idea of a 'budget', Dominic accepted the slip of paper and dropped it onto the table as if it barely concerned him at all. Seeing the gesture, Sophie felt her stomach execute an anxious cartwheel. Indignant that he hadn't even glanced at what she'd written, she sat back down on the couch with definite trepidation.

'You're not even going to look at it?'

'Later.'

What did he mean, 'later'? Wasn't that why he'd invited her round in the first place? To discuss ideas for a present?

'About the coat...' Dominic began.

Hot colour poured into Sophie's cheeks. 'What about it?'

'Did you even try it on?'

She was ashamed to silently admit that she had. It had felt wonderful, too—a perfect fit. She'd loved the way the expensive fabric had swished round her legs and made her feel like a million dollars. But there was no way she was going to let him know that.

'The point is, Mr Van Straten—'

He couldn't believe she'd referred to him so formally. *Why was she now trying to erect fences between them when they had already been so intimate?*

'Dominic. We surely know each other well enough to use first names?' he interceded smoothly.

Startled blue eyes met slightly mocking green ones, then quickly glanced away again.

'We hardly know each other at all! Despite...despite

what happened between us. I told you on the phone that I couldn't—*wouldn't*—accept the coat. What happened, happened, and now we should both just forget about it. Diana is married and on her honeymoon, and hopefully having a good time. That's all that matters now.'

'Do something for me, Sophie, if you will? It would please me greatly if you tried on the coat.'

To Sophie's astonishment he was taking it out of the package and holding it out to her by the shoulders, ready for her to slip into, as though nothing she'd said previously had got through to him at all. The idea—the very *thought* of letting him help her on with his expensive unwanted gift was tantamount to agreeing to strip naked in front of him. Sophie blanched.

'Dominic, I—'

'What is it, Sophie?'

'I don't want to try on the coat!'

'Why not? What can it hurt?'

'Are you always this persistent?'

'When I want something badly enough…yes.'

'Oh, this is just too ridiculous for words!'

Seeing that he clearly had no intention of discussing anything else until she submitted to trying on the coat, Sophie suddenly felt very foolish at making such a fuss. He was right. What *would* it hurt? She could slip it on quickly, remind him she had no intention of accepting it, then take it off again and insist that he kept it. After that, she could make her excuses and leave.

But as Sophie grudgingly got to her feet and stepped around the table towards Dominic, turning at the last minute so that he could slip the garment onto her shoulders, she was so overwhelmed by him that she felt herself tremble. His heat and his nearness, and the dynamic, powerful presence he exuded as easily as some men wore cologne, was a heady cocktail for any woman. The effect it had on her was like some kind of powerful opiate that sent her spinning off into a whole other stratosphere.

As he settled the material around her, her trembling would not cease, and she was mesmerised as, with his hands either side of her arms, he directed her slowly round to face him. Something in his eyes transfixed Sophie, and bolted her feet to the floor. A scorching look so hot and desirous that beneath the luxurious coat she'd reluctantly tried on for his benefit, her limbs had all the strength of cotton wool.

Dominic was staring at her mouth. With the barest hint of raspberry lipstick, her pretty lips were temptingly ripe and plump, and too inviting for words. Knowing the delights that they promised, he wanted to plunder them, taste them, *ravish* them, until a rising tide of passion swept over them both, consigning them willingly to a little divine madness that they wouldn't soon forget. Lust rose up inside him so strongly that for a moment it was all Dominic could do to remind himself that if he capitulated to such desire Sophie would—in all likelihood—run a mile, and never see him again.

Or would she?

Realising that she was trembling, and that the blue irises of her lovely eyes had turned fascinatingly dark, Dominic quickly reassessed his opinion. She wasn't as *immune* to his attraction as she clearly wanted to convey. His little brunette spitfire still desired him as much as he desired her—only she was apparently determined to ignore it.

The knowledge ignited an almost dizzying satisfaction deep inside him—a victorious gratification that right then gave him far more pleasure than any multimillion-dollar property deal. *He would have her in his bed again soon, and the result would be even more sensational and breathless than the first time; an electrical storm that would not so soon die out.*

Keeping his desire and his intention deliberately in check, Dominic stood back to admire Sophie wearing the beautiful cashmere coat. It suited her without a doubt, as he'd known it would, and all of a sudden he was determined that she should keep it—despite her protestations to the contrary.

'See how well it looks.' He led her over to the large gilt mirror above the marble fireplace and saw that a rosy hue had invaded her cheeks and heat had made her eyes sparkle. *The betraying heat of sensual awareness...*

Gazing back at her reflection in that huge mirror, unable to hide from the slowly dawning truth that her attraction for this man had deepened more than it had diminished, Sophie wondered how on earth she even kept her balance. Her shocking feelings had betrayed her, as if paying her *will* no intention at all. How had she come to find herself in such an unbelievable situation? With Dominic's hard-angled and handsome face staring at her from behind, his large square hands firmly on her shoulders in the luxurious coat so reluctantly donned, it was hard to think of anything except to recall how those self-same hands had felt when touching her bare skin. She almost swayed.

More affected than she wanted to be by her wild, racing thoughts, Sophie spun round, determined to make herself come to her senses. Stalking back to the couch, she felt a tide of embarrassed heat wash over her making her body feel awkward and too self-conscious to be natural.

'I've got to go. Really...I have to.'

The coat came off and she laid it over the arm of the couch. Then she straightened, and stared at Dominic with her arms folded protectively across her chest—if only to hide the fact that her aching, tingling nipples were fiercely pressing against the cool cotton of her bra, and would no doubt betray her desire more emphatically than words ever could.

'I want you to keep the coat.'

His voice was husky, clearly affected by the shocking charge of primal electricity that had just ebbed and flowed between them. His hooded emerald eyes looked drowsy and heavy...*aroused*.

'No.'

'Yes, Sophie. I bought it for you and I want you to have it.'

If she made any more fuss about the infernal coat she was going to embarrass them both, Sophie realised. Reluctantly, hesitantly, she picked it up, and stroked over the soft wool with the flat of her hand. 'Very well, then. I...thank you. But I want you to know that I don't make a habit of accepting expensive presents from men.'

'Good. Then perhaps I am the first? That pleases me. Now, tell me—do you have a boyfriend? Are you seeing anyone?'

Her mind whirling with all the possible implications of such an unexpected question, Sophie stared. 'No. But why should that—?'

'Come to my house for dinner tomorrow night. I will send Louis for you at seven-thirty.'

'I've already made you the list you wanted regarding Diana's present. Why do you want me to come for dinner?'

Dominic's arresting green eyes narrowed. 'Don't pretend to misunderstand me, Sophie. You know very well why I have invited you to dinner.'

The unspoken erotic tension that Dominic hinted at lay between them, hardly managing to stay beneath the surface of the polite civility they both struggled to maintain. Realising it, Sophie was genuinely terrified. She'd convinced herself that Dominic meant the gift of the coat as an insult to make her feel cheap, because she'd slept with him, and now she had to reassess the situation completely, because he seemed to be expecting something more from her than a one-night stand.

'You didn't invite me,' she retorted, her eyes bright with renewed indignation, welcoming the emotion to hide behind. 'You *ordered* me!'

'I do not particularly care how you interpret my invitation. I just want you to be ready when Louis comes to collect you at seven-thirty. Am I making myself clear?'

She saw then the steel that his business associates and clients must regularly come up against, and her knees threatened to buckle. When this man wanted something, was there anything or any*one* that would even *dare* to stand in his way? she thought in fright. Probably not, considering his vast wealth and influence in the world that he moved in.

Diana had mentioned on more than one occasion that when it came to property Dominic Van Straten had the same awesome expertise and authority in the arena as a certain renowned media tycoon had on newspapers. Sophie only had to glance round the room at the probably million-dollar paintings so liberally lining the walls to know that. The man was successful beyond imagining.

'You have made yourself perfectly clear. But nobody

orders me to do anything I don't want to do! Do I make *myself* clear?'

Dominic laughed, and Sophie's already compromised knees almost *did* give way at the sound. That laugh immediately and worryingly provoked fantasies of naked bodies entwined on sheets of pure luxurious silk and, to her consternation, Sophie found that the images she'd conjured up, were not so easily dispelled.

'All right, Sophie. Since you are so anxious to leave, I will let you go. But you will come back tomorrow with Louis at the time I suggested... Yes?'

She wanted to be able to rewind the tape. To go back in time to the moment she had given him Diana's list. If she could go back to that moment, Sophie knew with certainty that she would not have stayed or been persuaded to try on the coat. Not now she was only too aware that the powerful undercurrent of attraction that she was being propelled upon towards this man was too strong for her to fight.

Unable to deal with this new, highly unfair tactic of unbelievable charm, Sophie released a pained sigh, wondering what price fate would exact on her for relenting to such a crazy attraction for even a second. 'Just dinner, then. Afterwards I'll go home, and that will be that.'

'Do you think so?'

Dominic's voice was gently derisive, and a small shiver of delicious awareness, like a shower of soft summer rain, cascaded down Sophie's spine.

'I *do* think so.'

'Sophie?'

'What is it?'

She had reached the door, her hand about to grasp the doorknob. When she turned her head to glance back at Dominic he was smiling, and the sight of that arresting, ruthlessly in control, undoubtedly sexy gesture almost snatched her breath away. She knew he was using it to illustrate to her that *he* was the one calling the shots, not Sophie. She should have left, right then, not waited for him to speak.

'Tomorrow, please wear something a little more feminine to dinner. *For me.*'

Biting her lip, lest she retaliate with something *not* so 'feminine', Sophie left the room, and the house, without another word.

The following day Dominic flew to Manchester on business. He was negotiating a deal to purchase some premier land in the city, on which to build three blocks of penthouse apartments with prime views. In a bidding war with a rival developer, Dominic had done his homework, considering all the angles and loopholes where he might gain an advantage over his rival.

Maintaining his customary cool, he emerged from the meeting five hours later, with the deal tied up and a sharp appetite for lunch. He ate at one of the best restaurants in town, met for drinks afterwards with the heiress daughter of a wealthy friend—owner of that same restaurant and several others round the country—declined her hopeful offer of going on to somewhere 'a little quieter' afterwards, and jumped on a plane back to London.

Throughout the day, behind the sharp dealing and the ruthless determination to come out on top in a deal he'd decided months ago would be his, Dominic's thoughts had strayed briefly from time to time to Sophie. Every time they had done so, a warm buzz had filled his body, making him long for the day to draw to a close and slide into evening so that he could see her again.

It had been a while since the possibility of a heated

sexual encounter had filled him with such desire and anticipation—but then he had already had a taste of what was in store. Together, he and Sophie were combustible. *Even if the little schoolteacher seemed to resent him with a vengeance.* It would make her complete capitulation to their mutual desire all the sweeter. But, that said, it was not in Dominic's mind to rush things, like a bull at a gate. He would take it very slowly this time: tease her a little bit, play with her, harness in his own needs with just the right amount of check—so that after a while she would be as crazy in lust for him as he was for her...

By the time he arrived back at the house in Mayfair he was in a *very* good mood indeed.

CHAPTER FOUR

TWICE during the day Sophie had slipped out of school, once in the morning and again at lunchtime, to ring Dominic's phone number. Both times all she'd got was the response of an answering machine, and both times she had decided against leaving a message. To leave a message on his machine telling him that she was declining his dinner invitation after all seemed cowardly in the extreme, and would probably earn her nothing but his undying scorn. She had her weak points, but cowardice was not one of them.

When Sophie reflected back on last night she could hardly believe that she'd been so hypnotised by the man that she'd agreed to see him again. Now, when she thought about it in the cold light of day, the whole idea seemed like madness. A disturbing and hot sexual attraction had briefly taken the edge off her dislike, and had hoodwinked her into thinking she'd actually like to experience more of the same with this enigmatic man. An extremely wealthy and powerful man, so far above her up the ladder of success that Sophie couldn't even see the soles of his shoes.

They were so mismatched it was laughable! She couldn't even afford to replace her clapped-out old car with a second-hand one, much less jet off to another part of the globe at the drop of a hat. And as well as the chasm-size gap in their social conditions, she didn't even *like* him. She really didn't. She told herself the only reason he was interested in her in any way was probably because he saw her as grateful and an easy conquest. Now and again perhaps he thought it a novelty to slum it a little, with girls from 'downtown' instead of 'uptown'. No doubt he played such games with women all the time…just because he could.

No. The more Sophie deliberated on the matter, the more she was utterly convinced she should just tell him to his face that she wasn't interested.

If only she'd told him that she *did* have a boyfriend. But lying was not something that came naturally to Sophie, either—even if it meant protecting herself from billionaire predators like Dominic Van Straten. So she decided she would go with Louis at the appointed time, when he came to collect her, then ask if Dominic could come to the door and confront him head-on with the fact that she'd made a mistake in agreeing to see him again, that she'd thought about it, but decided it wouldn't be a good idea.

Feeling pleased with the innate good sense of her proposal, Sophie returned to her class of enthusiastic five-year-olds, and threw herself with relish into an afternoon of finger painting.

A soft spring rain was falling as Sophie waited outside Dominic's front door that evening. He'd asked her to wear something feminine, but beneath her ordinary black coat—she'd deliberately not worn the one he'd gifted to her—she was wearing a plain, nondescript black sweater and jeans. She had not dressed up at all. What was the point when she'd only gone there to tell him that she'd changed her mind?

But when Dominic answered the door himself, filling the very air with the force of his charisma and looks, arrestingly handsome in a black tuxedo, his light-coloured hair gleaming beneath the chandelier-lit entrance hall behind him, Sophie's resolve about not seeing him again was swiftly blown away, like fragile autumn leaves clinging precariously to a branch.

'I won't come in,' she started, flustered by the fact she'd deliberately dressed down. 'I only came to tell you that I won't be joining you for dinner after all. In the cold light of day I've had some—I've had some doubts.'

Her cornflower-blue eyes were enormous in her pale oval face, and the rain had bestowed a myriad of crystals in her glossy black hair. Disappointment cut a deep swathe through Dominic's chest, along with fury that she should reject him so easily. And underlying both those emotions was a desire that could hardly be contained. He'd waited all day to see her again, and now she was telling him that she had some 'doubts'. No woman had ever rejected his advances before, and he was adamant that Sophie wasn't going to be the one to ruin such a long-standing record.

'Come in,' he told her, holding the door wide. 'You're getting wet, standing out there in the rain.'

Turning down her coat collar, Sophie reluctantly stepped inside. The warmth and light of the magnificent entrance hall enveloped her in a different world entirely from the one that denoted her own daily existence. Great wealth had a certain 'scent', she decided, even without all its more obvious trappings. And Dominic Van Straten exuded that scent.

As he closed the door and turned back to study her, his green eyes assessed her figure as thoroughly as if she were a painting he was considering buying, then hovered with slow deliberation on her face.

'I have friends waiting to meet you, Sophie,' he remarked, indicating the closed double doors of the drawing room at the foot of the beautiful winding staircase. 'Will you deprive them of your company as well?'

'Friends?' Sophie repeated in alarm, astonishment making her light-headed. 'But I thought that it would be just you and—' Biting off the end of her sentence as Dominic narrowed his emerald gaze with a slightly mocking glint, she swallowed hard. 'You didn't tell me it was a formal invitation.'

Her cheeks went from alabaster-pale to a vibrant rose-red in the space of just a few short seconds. Her unspoken belief that Dominic had been planning dinner for just the two of them hovered treacherously in the air, making Sophie feel like the biggest of fools there ever was.

'Were you hoping it would just be the two of us?' Soft-voiced, Dominic alarmed her even further by moving closer to her, so that Sophie was suddenly on intimate terms with every straight blond eyelash and each beautifully carved plane and angle of his arresting face.

He smelled good too...too good. Under siege, her heart began to race.

'No!'

Denying the charge with a passion, she wished the opulent marble floor would do her a huge favour and part like the Red Sea beneath her feet. Anything to save her further ghastly embarrassment beneath this man's all-seeing, mocking gaze.

'I wasn't ''hoping'' for anything. Would I have come here to tell you that I was declining your invitation if that was the case?'

'I'd like you to stay, Sophie.' He said this in such a way that Sophie had no doubt that it was practically an order.

But there was no way on earth that she wanted to meet

his more than likely equally well-heeled friends dressed as if she'd just walked out of a dusty classroom…which she practically had. There were even stubborn traces of coloured paint left under her fingernails from her afternoon with the children! Remembering, Sophie curled her hands and immediately dropped them down beside her.

'I really can't. Thank you for asking, just the same, and for—for sending Louis to collect me. I didn't want to just leave a message, you see. I wanted to tell you in person.'

He admired her integrity, he really did. But he wasn't a man readily to concede defeat—no matter what the odds. Not when he knew for a fact that the little school-teacher was fighting as strong an attraction as he was. She was scared, that was all.

'Let me take your coat.'

To Sophie's astonishment, he worked his way deliberately down her buttons, popping open each one through its matching buttonhole with consummate ease. 'Dominic, I told you that I wasn't planning on staying!'

Impenetrable green eyes surveyed the plain black sweater she wore beneath her coat, the thin material hugging her breasts in a way that drew attention to the delightfulness of her shape. At the bottom edge of her sweater about half an inch of taut sexy midriff was on display above the plaited tan belt of her jeans, and Dominic's admiration intensified immediately. The outfit she was wearing might not scream designer chic, or be the most 'feminine' of clothing he could envisage, but he couldn't deny it was as sexy as hell.

'And I'm not dressed for dinner… You can see that!'

'You'll soon discover that being a friend of mine brings with it a certain amount of licence, Sophie. No one will bat an eyelid.'

Even if Sophie had believed him, which she didn't, walking into his grand drawing room looking as if she hadn't even bothered to think about what she was wearing, was not something she would do willingly. If any of his guests were women—and they were bound to be—of *course* they would bat an eyelid. They'd probably think that Dominic had seriously taken leave of his senses—entertaining a nobody like her, who couldn't even trouble herself to dress properly for dinner.

'I don't think so. If you knew how women can be, you wouldn't say that.'

'I do know women, I can assure you, and the only thing they will be is envious of your youth and beauty.'

About to protest, Sophie clamped her mouth shut, her pulse skittering as Dominic leant down and brought his face within the merest inch of hers. Closing his eyes, he deliberately breathed her in, his seductive cologne and body heat stirring the tiny space that separated them, making every tiny hair that covered Sophie's skin stand on end.

It was agony being so close, not free to touch him as she longed to, and for a dangerous second she almost raised her hand to stroke it down the side of his face. But he opened his eyes before that happened, and glinted down at her as though he could set her passion alight with just a glance. *Which he could*, Sophie admitted silently, again secretly admiring the generous blond lashes that gilded those amazing eyes of his.

'Andrews!' he called out, suddenly stepping back, and the manservant who had answered the door to Sophie yesterday appeared from a side door and walked smartly across the marble floor towards them.

'Yes, Mr Van Straten?'

'Take Miss Dalton's coat, if you please.'

'Dominic—I told you, I'm not staying!'

'I *want* you to stay,' he told her firmly, even as he helped her out of her coat and handed it to Andrews.

'What about what *I* want?' she asked feebly, feeling as if she were standing on stage, with a single spotlight trained deliberately on her and every vulnerable emotion and gesture brutally exposed for public delectation.

Glancing down at her figure-hugging jeans, she wished she had at least put on a skirt. But it was too late now, and anyway it was her own fault that she found herself in such a dilemma. She should have been firmer with Dominic. She should have—

'This way.'

Sliding a possessive arm around her waist, he led her towards the ominous double doors. And although Sophie vehemently wanted to resist his persuasion to accompany him into that room she found herself curiously unable to do so. It was as though her very will had somehow taken up residency somewhere else.

They entered to find Dominic's guests standing around with drinks in their hands deep in the throes of conversation. Their animated faces clearly denoted their enjoyment, and the sight immediately made Sophie feel excluded from that elite little circle. She knew instantly that even though she stood at Dominic's side she wasn't like them in any way. She didn't move in the same privileged strata that they did, and even if she'd had the inclination or desire to convince them differently both her obvious unease as well as the way she was dressed would reveal her to be a usurper.

As several heads turned towards her she longed to break free from Dominic's light hold on her waist and escape. But it was too late for that.

'This is Sophie, everyone. She dropped by to tell me

she was declining my invitation to dinner, but as you can see I've managed to persuade her to stay.'

Immediately taking umbrage at the surprising frankness with which he explained both her presence and her somewhat casual appearance, Sophie was nevertheless glad that at least now explanations for her attire would hopefully not be required. As to an explanation of what she was doing there at all—well, she would just have to pray that people would respect her privacy.

But, enduring the not-inconsiderable speculation in the glances of Dominic's other well-dressed guests, she seriously doubted it. Someone passed her a glass of wine from a tray and she glanced up and smiled her thanks. The man who'd undertaken the task was distinguished-looking, about fifty, and could not conceal the open curiosity in his frank gaze.

'I must say Dominic has kept very quiet about you, little Sophie. Where on earth did you two meet?'

'At a wedding,' Dominic interceded, the look in his eyes plainly conveying to Sophie that he would take care of things.

'Oh?' The man quirked an interested eyebrow. 'Someone we know? I heard that Lord Barrington's daughter Jemima got married to some stockbroker in the City the other week. Emily and I didn't go, of course. We were in Barbados for Roddy's twenty-first.'

As other people came to join their little group, the conversation proceeded, concerning people Sophie neither knew nor cared to know, their names bandied about like upmarket confetti and the mostly superficial exchange of words absolutely convincing her that she didn't belong there. Either with Dominic himself *or* his upper-class friends.

She found herself longing for the familiar and easy

comfort of her little maisonette, with her music playing on the stereo while she read or ate her dinner, her candles lit and her incense burning. The customary ritual was always a signal for her to shake off the cares of the day and relax. When a girl lived alone things like that became important cornerstones on which she could rely.

When she felt Dominic's hand clasp her own to his side, Sophie glanced up, startled to find him smiling back at her. The dimly lit lamps that burned in the room made his already arresting gaze even more troubling and unsettling to her peace of mind.

'Marcus was just asking what you do for a living, Sophie.'

'I'm a teacher,' she said clearly, her chin raised a little as if to say to the man standing opposite her, *Make of that whatever you will.*

'Lucky pupils,' Marcus remarked, laughing, but Sophie could find no humour in the condescending comment. 'What subject do you teach, Sophie?'

'A bit of everything,' She shrugged, and deliberately pulled her hand free from Dominic's. 'I'm a primary school teacher.'

'Of course. That makes sense.'

'What do you mean?'

'I only meant that you look far too sweet to be teaching big rough boys and girls, my dear. Don't you agree, Dominic?'

'Don't be fooled,' he replied, his green eyes openly teasing as they swept her indignant expression. 'She's a veritable tigress beneath that innocent little exterior.'

Gulping down a bit too much wine, Sophie sensed the alcohol delivering an intoxicating surge into her bloodstream, and for a moment her head swam.

'Dominic.' She addressed him, the expression in her

eyes as meaningful as she could make it. 'Could I have a word in private?'

'Certainly.' Without hesitation he slid his hand beneath her elbow, excused them both from his guests, and led her back outside into the entrance hall. 'What is it?'

Straight away Dominic knew that she was uncomfortable in his home, and was hating every second she had to spend with pompous individuals like Marcus. But Marcus's wife Emily was a warm, very liberal person, who accepted people just as they were, and she'd been a good friend of Dominic's for years. Unfortunately Emily had had to decline dinner at the last minute, and now Dominic wished he had put off the little dinner party he'd spontaneously arranged in preference for taking Sophie out to dinner or merely entertaining her on his own at home.

'I really can't stay for dinner. I have to go.'

'You mean you don't want to be here?'

Reddening a little round her jaw, Sophie spied a small table a couple of feet away and went to stand her wine glass on it. When she straightened again, Dominic was watching her intently, his expression unsmiling.

'Your friends aren't exactly my kind of people,' she told him. 'You must know that. I don't have a thing in common with any of them.'

'You sell yourself short, Sophie. You are a schoolteacher—an educated woman. Surely it is not beyond you to engage in a little meaningless conversation for…what?…a couple of hours at most?'

'Look, Dominic… I'm *tired*. I've had a busy day, and all I really want to do is put my feet up and unwind a little. It was kind of you to invite me to dinner, but, like I said when I first arrived, I had my doubts all along.'

He didn't want her to go. Now that she was here, with

her very tempting little body and her enormous blue eyes causing almost painfully acute little parries of desire throughout his body, Dominic wanted to keep her there. Once again he silently cursed his decision to have the dinner party instead of keeping Sophie all to himself.

'When can I see you again?'

His question, direct to the point of bluntness, completely took Sophie by surprise. *Was he serious?* Or was he only pursuing her because since they had slept together she had seemed to cool towards him?

'I'm sure you must be a very busy man. I think I—'

'I am not interested in discussing my schedule with you, Sophie. You can no doubt understand my frustration that this evening has not proceeded as well as I'd hoped. If you tell me when you are next free, I will *make* time for us to meet.'

A tiny muscle throbbed in his forehead, denoting a surge of emotion that surprised Sophie. As she studied his dauntingly good-looking visage, a fierce awakening of need and want throbbed through her body and made her head spin. She *did* want to see him again, because even when she wasn't with him she could not stop her incessant daydreaming about him. More than just a little overwhelmed by his highly potent charms, nevertheless Sophie instinctively knew that she had to protect herself—by keeping that knowledge to herself.

'Friday night,' she told him, rubbing her suddenly chilled arms. 'I'm free Friday night.'

'What time do you finish school?'

'What do you mean?'

'When do you finish teaching on Friday? I will come with Louis to pick you up. I have a meeting at a hotel in Suffolk from six until eight. I have already planned to stay there on Friday night. You can stay with me.

You can take a leisurely bath, get ready, and then we can dine together at around eight-thirty. What do you think?'

What do I think? Sophie silently repeated in panic. *I think I've just discovered a completely reckless side to myself that I didn't know existed until now! Surely I must be crazy to agree to spend another night with this man?* And not just *any* man. A man who could not only *buy* the hotel they'd be staying in a hundred times over, but who was completely out of her league in every way! *And what will Diana say when she finds out?*

'Dominic...I appreciate the invitation, I really do, but—'

'You are not going to turn me down?'

She could see immediately that the idea was anathema to him. Of all the women he could see, why had he picked on Sophie? She just couldn't understand it. Okay, so they had practically set the sheets on fire in bed together, but she didn't kid herself. For Dominic it was probably a regular and commonplace occurrence. He must meet beautiful women all the time.

It wasn't that she didn't value herself, or that she was putting herself down. It was merely Sophie's belief that men like Dominic Van Straten, who could have every single thing their heart desired—including their pick of stunning women—weren't generally known for dating ordinary, unassuming primary-school teachers. And especially not ones who lived in a run-down part of London and occasionally grabbed a Pot Noodle for lunch to eat on the run because they were either too busy or simply too disorganised to arrange anything else.

The kind of women that Sophie fully believed inhabited Dominic's world would eat in fancy restaurants and nibble lettuce leaves to keep their weight down. They'd go to plastic surgeons in Harley Street and have Botox and any number of nips and tucks to stay beautiful. But, regarding Dominic now, his emerald eyes blazing back at her with undisguised need, Sophie suddenly ran out of excuses to turn him down. The scary truth was, she didn't *want* to turn him down. No matter how unsuitably matched they were in reality.

'You really want to pick me up from school?' she asked, tucking a glossy dark curl behind her ear.

Dominic allowed his shoulders to relax. Relief ebbed through him with force. 'I am not accustomed to saying things I don't mean, Sophie.'

'Well...' Sophie shrugged. 'I don't know what my colleagues are going to think when you turn up in that chauffeur-driven car of yours on Friday.'

A genuinely amused smile curved her lips at the thought.

'Do you mind what they think, Sophie?'

Staring back at him, her smile disappearing as sensual heat flared hotly inside her, Sophie shook her head. 'No,' she admitted, defiance making her lift her chin. She didn't tell him then that she generally held herself a little apart from her colleagues, and didn't believe in gossip or getting too friendly. 'It's none of their business what I do or who I see outside of school hours.'

'Good.'

'I have to go now.'

'So you said.' Dominic's eyes glittered, as if he would hold her there and make her stay with just the sheer force of his will alone.

'Three-thirty,' Sophie told him, suddenly both nervous and enthralled at the idea of seeing him again, and spending the night with him on Friday.

'What?' He looked at her like a man who'd just woken up from a very erotic dream.

'You asked what time I finish…it's three-thirty.'

'I'll find Andrews and get your coat.'

As Sophie watched Dominic stride down the hall ahead of her, she couldn't help admiring the broad, undoubtedly muscular shoulders beneath his tuxedo, and the tall, imposing bearing that exuded such innate authority. A little frisson of pleasure danced down her spine and made her hug her arms tightly across her chest as her nipples tingled in guilty sexual awareness. It was hard to believe, but she suddenly found herself realising that three-thirty on Friday afternoon just couldn't come quickly enough…

CHAPTER FIVE

HURRYING out of school, with a heavy knapsack weighing down her shoulder and carrying her overnight bag, Sophie saw the car, its Rolls Royce insignia at the head, gleaming and stately, waiting by the kerb. Her heart skipped a beat, then, before she could catch her breath, promptly skipped another one.

Catching a glimpse of Louis behind the wheel, Sophie wondered if Dominic was observing her from behind those tinted windows at the back, and self-consciously slowed down. The last thing she wanted to appear was eager, and the only reason she had been hurrying was that she was actually ten minutes later than she'd said she would be.

Just before she reached the car, a colleague of Sophie's—a maths teacher called Barbara Budd—caught up with her, her curious gaze clearly trying to work out whether the gleaming vehicle had anything to do with Sophie.

'So, what are you up to this weekend Sophie?'

'Going to see friends. How about you?' Feeling a rush of colour flood her cheeks, Sophie tried to appear nonchalant, but guessed by the speculation still mirrored in Barbara's inquisitive hazel eyes that she hadn't quite pulled it off.

'That's never your lift, is it?' the other woman persisted, ignoring the question.

'I'm sorry, Barbara, I have to go. I'm already late. Have a good weekend, won't you?'

Knowing that her nosy colleague was still observing her as she reached the car and Louis stepped out to relieve her of her bags, Sophie wished that Dominic had chosen a less conspicuous place in which to wait for her. The street that the little Church of England primary school was situated in was hardly home to the kind of expensive vehicles that inhabited a billionaire's world, and no doubt it wasn't just her colleague Barbara who was looking on and wondering. On Monday morning, no doubt, the teachers' staffroom would be rife with gossip about Sophie's lift on Friday.

The car door on the passenger side opened kerbside. Dominic leant out to survey her coolly and Sophie got even hotter. 'You're late,' he said finally, his impervious green gaze travelling over her figure in the long black skirt, boots and sheepskin jacket.

Was he annoyed? Had he changed his mind about wanting her to join him on this trip? Sophie hovered on the pavement, furious with herself for capitulating to her ridiculously inappropriate need to see him again—and convinced now that the social gulf between them was far too wide ever to be bridged.

'The headmaster wanted to see me about something,' she explained, her pulse racing as his handsome face continued to study her from the car.

'Nothing serious, I hope?'

'Oh, no. He just wanted to warn me about reading subversive literature to my five-year-olds.'

Seeing the sudden confusion on Dominic's face, despite her anxiety, Sophie couldn't help but grin. 'I'm only joking.'

'Very amusing. Why don't you get in the car, then we can go?'

Did he have a sense of humour? As Sophie settled

back into the luxurious hide seat, her gaze re-acquainting itself with all the seductive features of that incredible car—from the burr walnut veneer to the deep-pile carpets and rugs beneath her feet—doubt overwhelmed her. At that moment she honestly would have jumped out of the car again had Dominic not smiled at her. That smile of his would have made the ground beneath her feet disappear if she'd been standing. The heat it stirred in Sophie's body started from the tips of her toes and ended in a series of fiercely electric tingles in her scalp.

'Did you have a good day?' he enquired politely, the man himself a sensory experience that far outweighed the seductive attributes of the famous car.

'Busy and...noisy,' Sophie grinned. 'Have you ever spent a day with a group of enthusiastic, chattering five-year-olds?' But even as she spoke, her lips had turned strangely numb, and she couldn't have said whether her smile would appear to him as a grin or a grimace. All she knew was that Dominic seemed to have a kind of explosive effect on her that she'd never experienced with another man before. From the tips of his expensive hand-made-leather shoes to the top of his silky blond hair he was in a class all of his own. A very *expensive* élite class.

Telling herself to try and relax, Sophie knew there was fat chance of any such thing if she continued to react as jumpily as a cat walking on burning coals around him.

'No,' he said without a smile. 'I have never spent a day like that.'

Relieved that she hadn't backed out of their arrangement, Dominic relaxed in the passenger seat next to Sophie and contemplated the drive and the evening ahead. He didn't know how such an unexpected, un-likely thing had come about, but he was feeling as smitten as a moonstruck youth with a severe case of unrequited lust around Sophie Dalton. All day he had anticipated her appearance with quietly excited stirrings deep in his belly, refusing to imagine for one moment that she would disappoint him and let him down at the last minute. After all, most women would jump at the chance of going on a date with him.

If doubt had surfaced at all he'd quickly and determinedly tried to bury it—yet, frankly, in all his thirty-six years Dominic had experienced nothing like the uncertainty he was presently suffering over this woman. And beneath the deliberately cool façade that belied the intense excitement running like a powerful river through his veins, Dominic *loathed* that uncertainty like nothing else.

For a man who was used to winning million-dollar deals before breakfast with stunning ease, feeling all at sea with a woman was not something he was used to at all. Having had the added advantage of being the progeny of already wealthy parents, even before he'd made his own fortune, Dominic had been used to the delights of the opposite sex since he'd been sent as a sixteen-year-old schoolboy to a prep school in England. Basically, he'd only had to cast his gaze at a pretty girl for her to fall at his feet.

Growing into a fully adult male, with the allure of not only handsome Viking-blond good looks but also wealth, dating women had been akin to being let loose in a treasure trove of sweet delights and told to help himself. It had been almost impossible to pick just one when there was always the enticement of several more should the flavour start to wane.

However, as Dominic's business acumen had honed into a more and more lethal skill, and the challenge of becoming one of the most successful property developers in the land had taken over, he'd mostly replaced his fascination for beautiful women with his work. For almost two years now he had been relationship-free, and had not minded the fact terribly much. Out of necessity he'd occasionally satisfied his healthy libido with a purely sexual encounter or two, but basically he actively welcomed the lack of distraction and demands of a relationship, if the truth were known.

But now, as his quietly ravenous gaze examined Sophie's beguiling profile, noting with pleasure the fierce sheen on her short ebony-black hair and the delicate turquoise studs in her perfect ears, Dominic was assailed by a wave of need so strong that it was almost beyond endurance.

His assistant, Diana, had often mentioned her friend Sophie, in passing conversation, but she'd never given him the slightest clue that the woman's appeal would be as dangerous to his equilibrium as it was. Now all Dominic could think of was the time he'd wasted being oblivious to her existence, when he could have been indulging in the passionate sensory delectation of having the sexy little teacher in his bed...

'Why Suffolk?' she asked him now, as she opened the buttons on her jacket and slipped it off in the warmth of the car.

For a moment Dominic honestly could not think straight. By rights, a plain red polo-necked sweater had no business being as alluring as satin and lace lingerie, but on Sophie it was. The soft wool clung to her breasts, outlining their undoubted perfection in a way that could trap a man's breath deep inside his chest. Dominic swallowed hard before he could get his lips to work.

'A client of mine I'm currently doing some business

with owns the hotel. The surroundings are picturesque, it's a lot quieter than London, and the food is first-class. Enough reason to hold our meeting there, wouldn't you agree?'

'It sounds…very nice.'

As Sophie folded her jacket and laid it across the fold-away armrest in the space between herself and Dominic her purse fell out of one of the pockets onto the lamb-swool rug that covered the floor. As she bent her head to retrieve it Dominic did the same, and for a timeless second, as their gazes met and held, Sophie was swamped with exhilaration and longing. Feeling the car start to glide away from the pavement, and the softly discreet hum of the engine helping to cocoon them in a private world all of their own, Sophie couldn't deny that it was one of the most sensually charged moments of her whole life.

He wanted to kiss her. How he'd held back from doing so Dominic didn't know, but in the space of just a couple of electrifying seconds he had fantasised hotly about melding his lips with hers. About commanding her to open her mouth. About becoming intimately acquainted once more with her sweet, entrancing flavours as only a lover dared.

If they had been anywhere else other than in his car, with Louis driving—in his apartment or his house, maybe—he would have definitely persuaded Sophie out of a few items of her clothing as well. As it was, they *were* in his car, with Louis driving, and so—painfully, and with great difficulty—Dominic willed his over-whelming desire back to a more manageable notch on the dial, and picked up Sophie's purse instead. As he handed it to her he saw a telling hint of red stain her smooth cheeks, and he sat back in his seat, intoxicated and enthralled by the brief sexual encounter, anticipating more, *much* more of the same, as soon as they could be alone together.

Telling herself that she might as well make the most of the wonderfully old-fashioned yet exquisitely appointed hotel room housed in this lovingly restored Tudor building on the edge of a timelessly beautiful Suffolk village, Sophie stripped off her clothes and immediately took a long, leisurely soak in the claw-toothed bathtub.

Dominic was going straight from his room to his meeting, and she wouldn't be seeing him again until eight-thirty, when they'd agreed to meet in the dining room for dinner. It gave Sophie some much-needed time to ponder how she was going to handle this unexpected excursion of hers into the lifestyle of the seriously rich. She knew that Dominic was fully expecting to sleep with her—why else would he bring her here?—but just for a second or two could she help it if her foolish heart longed for him to find pleasure in her company as well? She desired him, too. Just the thought of him *kissing* her again, never mind doing anything else, gave her serious goosebumps. But at the same time she wanted to make it clear to him that this wasn't the kind of encounter she indulged in on a regular basis.

She'd had her share of boyfriends—what young woman of twenty-six hadn't?—but Sophie had only gone 'all the way' with one of them. *Stuart.* And he had repaid her trust and devotion by having a drunken one-night stand with his best friend's girlfriend. Even though he'd begged her to forgive him, and had sworn to her that it would never happen again, Sophie had been unable to either forgive or believe him.

She'd told herself time and again that the experience

hadn't scarred her, that it had only made her naturally wary of involvement with men, yet beneath her brave assertions she knew that it *had* left its mark. Why else had she not seen anyone else for over a year now? She wasn't being conceited when she recalled that she'd had plenty of opportunity to meet other men. She'd even been asked out by two of the younger male teachers at her school. Yet *fear* of committing to another relationship had underscored every potential foray into that volatile, uncertain arena. *Until now.*

But Sophie wasn't some naïve schoolgirl. She knew with absolute certainty that Dominic wasn't likely to be looking for a relationship with her...just a hot little sexual dalliance in a hotel room to satisfy the itch of a rich man's fancy...

When nine o'clock came and went, and Dominic had still not appeared in the dining room to join her for dinner, Sophie picked up the paperback she had automatically popped into her handbag in case he was late and opened it at the page where she'd left her bookmark.

Endeavouring to concentrate on words that seemed to have the disconcerting ability to dance on the page, she couldn't get into the story no matter how hard she tried.

When the waiter appeared five minutes later and presented her with Dominic's apologies, explaining that his meeting had unfortunately run over time and that she should go ahead and order without him, Sophie put down her book with relief. Casting a surreptitious glance around at the other diners, she reluctantly picked up a menu.

She had initially been starving, but now her stomach simply felt uncomfortable—knotted with nerves. The longer she had to wait for him the more tense she grew, and the more time she had to tell herself that coming here at all with the Dutch billionaire had been one horrendous mistake. But suddenly he was there beside her, gazing down at her with the practised smile of a man who sometimes had to bestow that gesture in the course of a day's work to appease professionally, yet who did it with little sincerity or pleasure.

Sophie's stomach sank to her boots as she realised he would probably rather be dining alone than having to entertain a woman he knew very little about. She'd chosen her clothes this evening with such care, too. There was only one really smart outfit in her possession: this little black velvet dress with a matching bolero jacket and a choker with a fake ruby. The red of the ruby contrasted dramatically with her sable hair and blue eyes which this evening Sophie had carefully emphasised with plum-coloured eyeshadow and black mascara.

'I am sorry I am so late. Have you ordered yet?'

As he pulled out the opposite chair, Dominic's remote, preoccupied glance flicked over Sophie's appearance with no sign of any obvious pleasure, and again her heart flooded with doubt at the wisdom of joining him.

'No. I was just about to look at the menu. Didn't your meeting go well?'

Her astute observation sent an acute shaft of surprise hurtling through Dominic's system. Usually he was able to disguise his feelings better…*much better*. But this evening he had allowed himself to be rattled by a rival who had more than once snapped at his heels, over the years, and the encounter had left a bad taste in his mouth, leaving him questioning the wisdom of ruthlessly pursuing endless success for success's sake alone. He had seen desperation and greed so baldly reflected in that other man's eyes that he had felt sick to his stomach.

Was that how *he* appeared to other people who were less outwardly successful than he was?

So, no. His meeting had *not* gone well. He most definitely had not welcomed the introspection that had been forced upon him. But now, as he allowed his gaze to settle fully on Sophie's pleasingly pretty features, briefly dipping to examine the modestly low-cut neckline on her dress, displaying a hint of softly rounded feminine flesh, he experienced a strong surge of profoundly sexual pleasure that wouldn't be denied.

'I make it a rule never to mix business with pleasure, Sophie, so we will not discuss my dissatisfaction at my meeting and potentially spoil our evening together. You look very pretty in that dress, by the way.'

The way he delivered the unexpected compliment made Sophie shiver. All her muscles tensed as though she'd just emerged from a steam room into the shock of icy-cold rain. The man undid her with his eyes and at the same time scared her rigid with the raw, unfettered desire she saw reflected in them.

'Thank you. I bought it last year in the sales…' *She could have cut out her tongue.* Confessing she'd bought her best outfit in a sale to a man of Dominic's wealth and calibre was akin to inviting him to lunch and taking him to a workman's café for a fry-up! Where was her mind? She wasn't sitting cosily with some close girlfriend, having a chummy little chinwag! She was in a five-star hotel dining room with a man to whom the word 'portfolio' clearly didn't mean a case to carry around amateur attempts at artwork!

'Nevertheless,' Dominic commented, unsmiling, 'it complements your colouring and figure very well.'

His coolly voiced reply did not help Sophie's discomfiture one bit. Her silly *faux pas* had merely been another illustration to point up the vast and untenable social distance between them. Suddenly she couldn't even find it in her heart to *pretend* to be hungry.

'I think I should just go home. You're clearly regretting asking me here, and to be honest it wasn't such a great idea in the first place. I'm a primary-school teacher who leads a very ordinary type of life, Dominic. I don't mix with the kind of people you mix with, and I know nothing of your world. I know I'm probably a bit of a novelty to you, but that doesn't do a hell of a lot for my confidence either. So, to save both of us from further embarrassment, it's probably just best if we call the whole thing off. Don't you think?'

The last few words came out in a heated rush, and Sophie blushed and glanced away as Dominic began to smile. This particular smile bore no relation whatsoever to the coolly professional one he had worn when he'd first come into the restaurant.

'You are labouring under a very misguided assumption indeed if you believe that I'm regretting asking you to join me. I very much want you to be here. Apart from my meeting this evening I have thought about nothing else all day. And you insult both yourself and me by suggesting that I think you are some kind of 'novelty'. I only date women who interest me, Sophie—and not just physically. I am not so shallow that I could endure unintelligent or boring conversation just for the sake of gazing at a pretty face! Although in your case I think I might be prepared to make an exception. *Especially* when we go to bed. Although of course I wouldn't expect us to be indulging in much conversation then.'

Sophie's already heated blush grew even hotter, making her feel as if she were being slowly grilled under a sunlamp. Her lower lip trembled.

'You have nothing to say to this?' he goaded.

It was rare that Sophie was at a loss for words, but she acutely felt at such a loss now. Her racing thoughts just couldn't seem to make a connection with her vocal cords. 'Then...then I should...*stay*?' she asked, small-voiced.

'You should *definitely* stay.' He smiled again, that lethal, unfettered, destroying smile of his, and casually picked up his menu.

Inside the hotel room the curtains had been drawn and it was dark. When she reached for the light switch Dominic immediately pulled her hand away before she could turn it on. His cologne and his sheer male heat whispered over Sophie's senses like a powerful sensory drug, making her feel oddly disorientated and boneless with need.

'I am glad we skipped dessert,' he said teasingly, sliding his hand round her nape and tilting her face up to his.

His warm breath softly skimmed her face, like the brush of a butterfly's wing, and Sophie wondered what had happened to the ground, because suddenly she didn't seem to feel it beneath her feet any more. She told herself it was the wine she'd drunk at dinner, but knew in her heart she would be just as intoxicated if not so much as a drop of alcohol had touched her lips. This man's presence made her feel *drunk* with pleasure, unravelled with need.

'Sexy little Sophie.' He smiled, and touched his mouth experimentally against hers.

It was a mere brush, but as soon as the unrivalled taste of him exploded on her lips Sophie groaned a little and opened her mouth beneath his. The unpremeditated movement was as natural and as essential to her as breathing. Dominic needed no further entreaty or encouragement from her to take what he so voraciously longed for. He dived in without apology or hesitation, captivating her with his tongue, his ministrations ruthlessly exquisite, making her drown in desire as he explored the softly velvet surfaces inside her mouth.

As his hands caressed Sophie's body, acquainting themselves unhindered with her breasts, her hips, her bottom, he cupped the cheeks of her derrière in his palms and pulled her hard against his own aching manifestation of desire. She was in no doubt that he wanted her, and wanted her with the kind of passion and ardour that made her legs almost buckle in disbelief.

She stumbled a little as he guided her across what seemed to be miles of plush deep-pile carpet to the large, inviting king-sized bed with its plump cream duvet and crisp cotton sheets which the maid had turned down for the night. She heard the rustle of clothing being removed as Dominic slipped out of his jacket, tore at the buttons on his silk shirt, and bent his head to her neck to suckle on her exposed flesh. Feeling his teeth nip her, she put her hands up to grab onto the broad muscular banks of his shoulders for fear of falling, barely registering that his hands were unzipping her dress and dragging it down her body along with her jacket.

Time seemed to slow, taking on an almost unreal quality. *Oh, God…since when had she become so terrifyingly weak in the face of a man's desire?* So weak that she'd consider giving him anything he wanted? *She didn't do this.* She didn't sleep with men on a whim— no matter how attracted she was. But the man guiding her purposefully onto the bed was no whim. He set her blood pounding in her veins, like a throbbing, searching river, making her ache for him right down to her very marrow.

Falling with her onto the bed, Dominic covered Sophie's trembling flesh with his hard, impressive musculature, making her body burn wherever it came into contact with his. He kissed her deeply and voraciously, impatiently releasing the fastening on her bra and just as impatiently disposing of the flimsy garment altogether.

Feeling cool air awaken the naked flesh of her breasts, teasing her nipples into stinging buds of acutely sensitive steel, Sophie reached up and wrapped her arms around Dominic's neck, then slid her fingers through the thick blond strands of his hair, silently thrilling at the sensuous contact. She was desperate to touch him, and her longing knew no bounds. Feeling hungry and daring, she let herself explore the tempting outline of his hard body, feeling the taut flesh of his buttocks tense beneath her eager hands and his burgeoning desire press ever closer into the apex of her thighs.

Barely able to contain his rapidly growing lust, Dominic found the silky scrap of lace she wore that passed for panties and, pushing it aside, slid his finger into the searing moist flesh between Sophie's slim thighs. She arched her body against him like a cat and he drove deeper, withdrew briefly, then continued his lustful exploration with two fingers. Her scent undid him, hitting Dominic hard with its powerfully provocative sensuality and its erotic promise of pleasure unmatched. So much so that he found himself shaking with need as he endeavoured to find the sealed condom he had slid into his trouser pocket and undo it with any kind of finesse. That he managed it at all was a miracle, and as he unfurled it onto the throbbing, aching length of his manhood he was almost dazed by the fierce, ravenous hunger that ruthlessly possessed him.

How could she entrap him so? he asked himself heatedly, as he positioned himself at her entrance and thrust inside. Her soft moans almost finished him there and then. *How could this slim, fiesty scrap of a girl turn him on almost past bearing?*

Right then, Dominic wasn't actually looking for answers. But as he lowered his eager lips to her exposed breasts, palming one as he suckled the other, filling her with every hard inch, he did wonder how he had survived without this amazing and wild gratification for so long.

The pleasure he had received from his previous sexual encounters was like a calm breeze in comparison to this stormy cyclone. How had he possibly been satisfied by such soulless forays when it was clear to him now that he had an ache inside him for profound contact with *passion* so deep that it scarcely bore thinking about? That he had accepted mediocrity in his love life, and had laid aside the search for something more compelling in preference to becoming more and more successful in his work, truly astonished him.

But now that he had much more of an insight into what he really wanted sexually, Dominic had no intention of relinquishing it any time soon. If Sophie imagined that this tumble in a hotel-room bed was the mere whim of a rich man who could have anything he wanted, then her assumption was very quickly and earnestly going to be proved wrong.

'Dominic,' she breathed wildly as she writhed beneath him. 'Dominic, you're making me crazy... I can't... I can't stop myself from...'

'Let go, Sophie.' Thrusting harder and deeper,

Dominic revelled in the sweet joy of feeling her velvet muscles enfold him, contracting fiercely again and again as though she would never let him go. Her gaze was stunned and her body trembling uncontrollably as Dominic lowered his mouth to hers once again. Then, with one more savagely possessive, searing thrust, he heard himself cry out in amazement and joy before sinking down onto her trembling figure, his hands combing through her short dark hair as tenderly as if she were someone very important to him. Her dewy skin was so soft and her body so warm and inviting that Dominic wanted to spend the whole night making love to her, extracting every drop of pleasure he could, knowing that even then his desire for her would not be sated.

'You are glad you did not go home?' he teased, his expression somewhere between a smile and a frown.

Had she ever been so acutely conscious of every single thing before? So minutely and exquisitely aware of her heart beating with such untrammelled delight? As though every molecule of air she breathed were infused with wonder? Closing her eyes momentarily, to stop herself from crying, Sophie knew she had not. It wasn't as though she had never experienced moments of great pleasure or joy either. It was just that she had never known what she had been missing, what her body had been secretly *yearning* for, up until now.

Dominic might be able to get up out of this bed and carry on with his life without feeling as though a glimpse of heaven had just been snatched away from him, but Sophie seriously had to wonder if she could do the same.

CHAPTER SIX

TO SAY he was surprised to wake up and find the space beside him in the bed empty again would have been to seriously understate the power of the shock that pulsated through Dominic at the realisation. Rising up out of bed, checking the bathroom and finding it empty, he could not believe that Sophie had not woken him but had got up, instead, showered, and gone about her day as if the very *thought* of his own needs or wants had not even crossed her mind. He was unaccustomed to such cavalier treatment by a female, and for long moments he couldn't contain his anger.

As far as his own memory of the night before went, they had made love until the early hours of the morning when reluctantly, but out of necessity, both of them had finally succumbed to sleep. Used to waking early, and knowing that he had some unfinished business from yesterday's unsatisfactory meeting to take care of, he'd fully intended to let Sophie sleep on undisturbed, then join her for breakfast at around nine. *Had he not told her as much?*

It was hard to deny his fury at the thought that she had rebuffed his suggestion, and now, as he paced the floor outside the cosy and intimate dining room, Dominic wished that he'd stated his desire for her company more firmly. His body throbbed and tingled in the aftermath of last night's wild and urgent passion, and he was impatient to see her again this morning.

But even as the thought surfaced, something told him

*that Sophie Dalton was a law unto herself...a woman
as surprising and unpredictable as a snowfall in summer.* He had—after all—pursued *her. Not* the other way
round, as was often the case as far as he was concerned.
But, that being true, Dominic was still anxious to assert
who held the upper hand in their fledgling relationship.
He was totally unaccustomed to being on tenterhooks
around a woman, and did not like it one bit. He certainly
did not intend to allow it in the future.

Sophie walked with her head down, barely noticing the
pretty white swans that swam in the river alongside the
lane that she was heading down. She barely noticed anything at all, in fact. Not even the luxurious scent of blos-
som that hung in the air—a perfume that she normally
revelled in, come the spring.

There was no way she could have faced Dominic
across the breakfast table this morning.

*Pass the marmalade, please—and, oh, by the
way...thank you for the three orgasms.*

An embarrassed groan escaped her as she walked.
What had she done? And what was she supposed to do
now, when she'd compounded the folly of sleeping with
him not just once, but *twice? And with such inhibition
and reckless passion too?*

She had no idea what was going to happen next. This
whole unbelievable scenario was so out of her day-to-
day experience that she barely knew what to think. She
had never slept casually with a man before simply for
sex, then walked away as if all they'd done was have
tea and a platonic chat together. How did some women
do that?

If her bags hadn't been back at the hotel she would
have found the nearest station and made her way home

by train. She could have left Dominic a note saying *thanks for a lovely evening and see you around some time*—or something equally casual, to let him know she was a woman of the world who understood this kind of lightning attraction that flared one minute and burned out the next.

Only Sophie had the niggling feeling that what she felt for Dominic wasn't very likely to burn out in an instant. In fact, the opposite was most likely true.

By the time she decided to head back to the hotel she couldn't honestly say she felt one bit better about things. The truth was, she was even more troubled than ever. *And what on earth was Diana's reaction going to be when she found out that her best friend had slept with her boss while she and Freddie were on their honeymoon?*

Her expression preoccupied as she pushed open the door and encountered the welcome warmth of the hotel foyer, Sophie didn't immediately see Dominic, sitting in a cosy alcove nearby drinking coffee and reading a newspaper. He, on the other hand, saw her instantly, and put down his paper and his cup of coffee and strode across the deep blue carpet towards her with unquestionable purpose.

'Did we not have an arrangement to meet at nine for breakfast?'

The admonishing glance he bestowed upon Sophie was so devoid of warmth that she literally shivered. *He looked so good, too.* Lean and muscular and handsome in his dark blue sweater and black jeans. For a moment she was completely distracted. Even though the clothes he wore were undoubtedly casual, they were stamped with an irrefutably expensive air that conveyed to whoever glanced his way that for their owner money was no object.

'You said you were going to work first! Anyway... I wanted to go for a walk, so I just had a quick cup of tea and a slice of toast. Sorry.'

'You might have asked me if I was in agreement with such a decision. When I make an arrangement I am not accustomed to having it broken without so much as a message to let me know that things have changed.'

He sounded so serious and irate that for a moment Sophie wanted to laugh out of sheer embarrassment. Not many people could make her feel like one of the five-year-olds she taught at school.

'And I am not accustomed to having to report my movements, or indeed ask for permission to go for a walk should I so desire!' Her blue eyes flashed up at him with little sparks of fury in their cornflower depths.

'I did not say that you needed to ask my permission. Where did you go?' Dominic caught the male receptionist throwing them an inquisitive glance, and sliding his hand beneath Sophie's elbow, deliberately moved her out of earshot, back to the alcove where his coffee and newspaper sat waiting.

Glancing resentfully back at him, Sophie shook her arm free of his hold and dug her hands deeply into the pockets of her coat.

'I don't know *exactly* where I went! To tell you the truth I didn't pay much attention to it. I just needed to get out and get some fresh air. Is that such a crime?'

'Do you normally overreact to such a simple and innocent question?' His calm voice—although tinged with irritation—made Sophie feel slightly stupid.

To tell the truth, she didn't *know* why she was reacting to him so badly. She only knew that she had no idea how to handle the passionate intimacy that had taken place between them. Even now, when there was obvious dissent between them, her breasts were tingling like crazy, wanting to have him touch them, to have him squeeze and pull and—

'Sophie?'

Heat suffused her in a gushing torrent, and she had to wrench her glance away before he read the pure naked need that she knew must be reflected in her eyes.

'I'm feeling a little on edge. I'm sorry.'

'Why don't you take off your coat and sit down? I'll order us some more coffee.'

Not answering, Sophie did as he suggested, leaning back into the soft velour chairback, the idea of coffee suddenly sounding like the best idea in the world. Her bloodstream needed a shot of something, that was for sure!

When Dominic returned to the alcove after speaking to the receptionist, arranging his fit, muscular body in the chair opposite with relaxed ease, Sophie was finally forced to face him. To be honest, she was surprised that he seemed to want to linger. On the way back from her walk she'd convinced herself that he would be more or less ready to leave and anxious to return to London when she got back. He was a busy man, in much demand, and clearly his time was at a premium. Or so Sophie believed.

'Perhaps you would like to tell me why you are so on edge?' he suggested calmly,

'I really don't have any experience of this kind of thing, if you want to know the truth. It's not something that I do very often,' Sophie responded, her voice soft. 'Well...I mean when I say not very often I mean—what I mean is...*never,* really.'

'You mean making love with a man you have only just met?'

Licking her lips, Sophie nodded.

'I am glad to hear it.'

There was definitely a proprietorial air in his tone, and Sophie's head snapped up in surprise. As Dominic studied her, trying vainly to tamp down the desire that was quietly but indisputably rising like sap in his veins, he experienced a sharp sting of jealousy at the mere idea of her sleeping with anybody else but him. It was an unfamiliar feeling for him, and for a long moment he simply let the thought sit and gather quiet purpose, running with it as he characteristically did when the excitement of a new challenge beckoned.

'But you have had boyfriends, yes?'

'Yes but I didn't—that doesn't mean that I—'

'Are you telling me that you need commitment before you sleep with a man, Sophie?'

That wasn't what she was telling him at all! Sophie thought, a little desperately. This was the very thing she had wanted to avoid! Dominic believing that she felt the right to make some kind of claim on him now, because they had slept together. She might not be a *femme fatale* by anybody's standards, but she wasn't completely naïve.

'I'm not telling you that at all. Can we change the subject?'

'You are uncomfortable talking about intimacy?'

Dominic couldn't believe she was actually blushing after what they had done last night! The observation made him warm to her even more…not to mention made him hungry to have her back in bed with him. Already in his mind he was rapidly going over his schedule for the week, trying to work out when and how soon he could steal a couple of hours away from matters of business to be with her.

'I think—Oh, coffee…great!' Saved by the sudden appearance of a slim young waiter arriving with their coffee, Sophie busied herself placing cups on saucers and arranging the sugar bowl and cream on the table in front of them. She sensed that Dominic's gaze very rarely left her, even to thank the waiter for the coffee, and tiny prickles of intense awareness skimmed up and down her spine in quick succession. 'Shall I pour?'

'Sophie?'

The glance he gave her was both insistent and commanding, and Sophie stopped fussing with the coffeepot and put it down again on the tray. When she returned his glance her eyes were very blue and very wide.

'What?'

'I am getting the impression that you believe that after today I will not want to see you again. Is that right?'

It was not only right but so spot-on to what she'd actually been thinking, at that precise moment, that Sophie had to shake off the uncanny feeling of someone walking over her grave.

'You must be a very busy man, Dominic. Diana told me that in the past year it's been rare for you to even be in the country for more than a week at a time. And I…I have a busy life too. Obviously not at the same high level that you do, but just the same…I don't really have time for relationships.'

'You don't have time or you are anti-relationships?' A blond eyebrow lifted speculatively towards his scalp.

Stuart. To give yourself to a man in the most intimate way and then find out that he could quite casually give himself to another woman when he was having a relationship with you—well…that was quite *unforgivable* in

Sophie's book. This betrayal had stung worse than a hundred razorblades slicing into her flesh. And if she wasn't in a hurry to risk the same thing happening again, could anyone honestly blame her?

The Dominic Van Stratens of the world were playboys. Men who changed their women as regularly as they changed their cars. It didn't matter that he had the power to set her body aflame with just a hot, hungry look. What mattered to Sophie was honesty and integrity in a man, and above all...reliability too. Women who would trade that for a brief passionate fling were asking for trouble, in her view. And she had just walked up to trouble and invited it in!

'It's not that I'm "anti-relationships". I just told you that I have a very busy life. Shall I pour the coffee now?'

Her hand shook slightly as she poured the steaming beverage into their cups. *He should be grateful,* she considered, with feeling. Grateful that she wasn't one of those women who would cling on to a tenuous association in hope of something more. He'd had his *fun.* Well...they had *both* had a good time in bed, Sophie admitted silently, feeling hot. Why couldn't he just leave it at that and stop quizzing her about relationships?

'You are wrong if you imagine that I do not want to see you again.'

The innate authority in his voice made Sophie glance up in surprise. His expression was very serious, and for a couple of disconcerting seconds Sophie remembered a very *different* expression...in the throes of his passion, when he had made her rejoice in her womanhood and gasp for joy as his hands touched her everywhere...

'I have commitments for the next three days, but I have a slot free on Wednesday evening. You can come to my house for dinner.'

Did he have any idea how cold and uninviting such a command sounded? As much as her body betrayed her at just the slightest touch from him, Sophie was not going to succumb to such an emotionless dictate, like some kind of eager little puppy.

'I'm not free on Wednesday,' she replied coolly, raising her cup to her lips. 'I'm working late at school, getting my classroom ready for Easter.'

Dominic felt impatience surge through his bloodstream like a cursed virus. Was she deliberately being difficult, or was she speaking the truth? For her to reply to his invitation as though she could easily take it or leave it—and in this case obviously *leave* it—made him furious. Did she have any idea how many women would love the chance to be alone with him, for just a few hours even? Clearly she didn't. But what got to Dominic even more was the idea that even if Sophie *did* know how much in demand he was by the opposite sex, it wasn't likely to sway her decision one jot. The woman must be obsessed by her job. That was the only explanation that made any sense to him.

'Well, what about Thursday evening?'

He had an invitation to meet a colleague for dinner at his club, but as far as Dominic was concerned right now his need to see Sophie was far greater.

There was still no warmth in his voice, and Sophie squirmed uncomfortably in her seat. She wouldn't go running to him just because he willed it! If he thought she was one of *those* weak-willed, infatuated females who would drop everything for a man, then he was definitely barking up the wrong tree!

'I'm going out on Thursday night with a girlfriend, to celebrate her birthday.'

It was perfectly true. But as Dominic sat glowering

back at her she knew he was convinced she was lying. He swore. At least Sophie *thought* he was cursing, because he'd suddenly switched languages as easily as breathing.

'So when *will* you be free again to see me?' he demanded, emerald eyes glittering.

Sophie almost choked on her coffee. Placing the cup back on its saucer, she smoothed her hand down her jeans and sat back in her chair in astonishment. 'To be frank with you, Dominic, I thought this must be a one-off. Well...I mean, I know it happened once before, but I realise that you're a very busy man, and that you wouldn't normally be seeing someone like me. Anyway... I thought... That is, I didn't—'

'Let me be clear about this Sophie,' Dominic interjected firmly. 'I don't think I'm being conceited when I say I know when a woman receives pleasure from my touch. I also don't think that I imagined your soft moans and sighs in my arms last night. That being the case, I believe you wouldn't exactly be against seeing me again. Am I right?'

Sophie sensed that he was probably completely unused to anyone turning him down when he wanted something. Most people in his life probably wouldn't *dare* turn him down. But, as much as Sophie disliked the idea that Dominic could have anything he wanted just by snapping his fingers, she couldn't deny her own heartfelt need to be with him again. And that need far outweighed her personal feelings about the power and authority he was used to. After all, in bed he was just a man. A man with the same passionate needs and desires as any man who had far less materially.

'I honestly can't make Wednesday or Thursday. How about next Friday?'

Some of the incredible tension that had gathered in Dominic's shoulders eased slowly out of his muscles. Relieved, he ran his hand round the back of his neck. 'Friday I'm presenting a business award at the Guildhall in London.'

'Oh.'

'It's black tie, so you will need an evening dress. Is that a problem?'

Knowing intimately the rather scant contents of her wardrobe, Sophie guessed the sudden panic in her eyes must be self-evident to Dominic. 'I might have to borrow something from a friend,' she confessed, embarrassed.

'I'll phone my friend Emily and ask her to take you shopping for a suitable dress. Give me your phone number before we part, and I'll get her to ring you to arrange a suitable time.'

'Dominic, I don't have time to go shopping! Much less money to splash out on an expensive dress. I'm sorry, but it's not the kind of item that a primary school teacher's pay will easily stretch to.' There...she'd said it. And now her embarrassment at such a confession to a man for whom money clearly *was* no object just grew ten times worse.

He smiled. 'Let me buy you the dress, Sophie. It would give me immense pleasure to do so.' His hypnotic gaze lingered on her mouth as he said this, then moved slowly and deliberately down to her breasts, outlined by her close-fitting sweater.

Sophie found it impossible to breathe for a moment.

'I told you, I don't make a habit of accepting expensive gifts from men.'

'I'm not just any man, Sophie. We both know that I am your *lover*.'

On Monday, on her return to school, the gossip and speculation in the staff-room proved to be even worse than Sophie had feared. Barbara Budd had not wasted any time in telling anyone who'd cared to listen that Sophie had been picked up on Friday by a chauffeur-driven Rolls Royce, and they all inevitably wanted to know why.

Insisting on her privacy, Sophie endured the seemingly unending curiosity until home-time, and then on her way out she bumped into Victor Edwards, the headmaster.

'I take it I can expect your resignation any day now?' he started, adjusting his dark-rimmed glasses on his nose as he glanced down at her from his more superior height.

Hardly able to believe her ears, Sophie almost stumbled on the last concrete step in the hallway that led to the exit. 'I'm sorry?'

'Well, Sophie, it's not every day that teachers go home in Rolls Royces. We are either paying you far too much—which is extremely unlikely, as we all know— or you are moving in the kind of illustrious circles that are sadly closed to the rest of us mere mortals.'

Sophie had a lot of respect for their strict headmaster, even if he could sometimes be what the other staff referred to as a 'stick-in-the-mud'. She'd always found him to be very fair, and not likely to make impulsive judgements when it came to any kind of trying or difficult situation. Now, as she tried to gauge whether he was serious or not, she breathed a sigh of relief as she saw a smile break around his rather austere lips.

'I am, of course, only joking about your resignation. You're one of the best infant-class teachers at the school, and I would be very sorry to lose you should you ever decide to leave us—even though I know you are eager for your career to progress. I'm sure you've been driven round the bend today, with all the silly gossip that's been going around. My advice is just to ignore it, Sophie. Tomorrow they'll all find a new topic to gossip about, and that will be an end to it.'

'Thanks for that, Victor. I must admit it's been quite trying, to say the least.'

'How are preparations going for Easter?'

'Great! The children have all been making Easter bonnets today and I've been up to my eyes in crêpe paper and glue!' Her big blue eyes shining, Sophie glanced back at Victor with unconstrained delight. A slight flush stained the man's otherwise pale cheeks at her enthusiastic response, and Sophie experienced a twinge of surprise at this uncharacteristic indication of emotion.

'You certainly have a way with the little ones,' he commented kindly. 'I suppose there must come a day when you'll decide to have a brood of your own?'

'Maybe…I don't know.'

Suddenly more discomfited by the thought than she cared to confess, because for an outrageous, impossible moment she'd allowed herself to imagine Dominic as the father of that 'brood', Sophie self-consciously tucked a curl of dark hair behind her ear.

'Not for a long time yet, though.'

'Good.' Victor proclaimed, nudging his glasses further up his nose and adjusting his briefcase under his arm. 'That seems a sensible decision, if you don't mind my saying so. Keep up the good work, and don't ever hesitate to come and talk to me should anything at school get you down.'

'Thanks.'

'Well, I'll see you tomorrow, then.' Without a backward glance, Victor preceded Sophie to the twin doors of the exit and marched out of the building.

Shaking her head at this unexpectedly warm exchange, Sophie couldn't help but smile as she made her way out of school to the bus stop a few streets away.

Wrapping a huge yellow bathsheet around her, and hurrying out of the bathroom to the ringing telephone in the living room, Sophie snatched up the receiver, her stomach muscles clenched tight in anticipation that the caller might be Dominic.

It wasn't. But it *was* someone connected with him. Emily Cathcart—the woman he'd promised would ring to arrange to take Sophie shopping for a dress for an occasion that frankly filled her with dread. It was one thing sharing a night of passion in an anonymous hotel with him. It was quite another going out in public as his escort—and to such a clearly important event.

Before she'd taken her bath Sophie had spent a good hour or more looking at every reference to Dominic Van Straten on the Internet. There were literally *pages* of stuff about him. He was a busy man. A much-sought-after and admired entrepreneur, and a property developer *bar none*. Not only was he in demand to *give* awards, if the information that Sophie had read was correct, he had been on the *receiving* end of plenty, too.

'Emily Cathcart, here. Am I speaking to Sophie Dalton?'

'Yes, you are.' Sinking down into a nearby armchair, Sophie adjusted the towel more securely around her chest and tried to ignore the disconcerting bump of her heart against her ribcage.

'Dominic asked me to contact you, Sophie,' the woman explained cheerfully, immediately taking charge. 'Now, when can we meet to go shopping? I'm free tomorrow lunchtime—would that suit?'

How would Emily Cathcart receive the news that Sophie had changed her mind about the whole thing? she wondered. *It wasn't Emily's reaction she had to worry about.* Dominic was the one who would probably go ballistic. Besides, it was far too short notice to tell him that she wasn't going to go with him now. He'd more than likely have made arrangements for dinner, and that kind of thing.

'I can't do tomorrow; Wednesday lunchtime would suit me better. It will give me a chance to make arrangements at school. I could probably get another member of staff to cover for me for a couple of hours.'

'Wednesday lunchtime it is, then. I'll come and pick you up if you tell me where you are.'

'You don't happen to drive a Rolls Royce, do you?' Sophie asked light-heartedly, grimacing at the very thought. At the other end of the phone Emily guffawed loudly, and Sophie immediately found herself warming to the woman she hadn't even met, yet.

'Good grief, no, darling! I drive a common or garden Range Rover, if you want to know. Comes in awfully handy when you live in the country, like me. Bit intimidating, was it? Dom turning up in his Rolls Royce outside school?'

Smiling at the memory, Sophie relaxed back into the chair. 'You could say that. If you knew the part of London where my school is, you'd know that Rolls Royces are just about as rare as hen's teeth!'

'Dominic told me you were a primary school teacher, and Marcus described you as a pretty little thing. My husband met you at Dominic's the other night, when you had to leave early. Shouldn't be too difficult to kit you out in something special for the do on Friday. Give me your address, and I'll see you there on Wednesday at one. How's that sound?'

'It's very good of you…Emily. Thank you.'

'Not a bit of it! Dominic and I are old, old friends. I'd do anything for him, and that's the truth, so it's really no hardship at all, my dear.'

CHAPTER SEVEN

SHE was late, and Dominic felt as jumpy as a man on Death Row as he glanced over the heads of the two guests who were monopolising him towards the entrance of the historical, chandelier-lit anteroom.

He'd wanted Sophie to accompany him in the Rolls, but she had insisted she would get a taxi and meet him at the Guildhall because she'd had to go to an unexpected staff meeting after school and didn't want to risk keeping him waiting should she be late.

Impatiently Dominic glanced at his watch. *Why hadn't she told them she couldn't make the staff meeting tonight of all nights?* Did *his* needs count for nothing? Biting back his irritation, because it was almost time to go in to the main dining room for dinner, he sipped uninterestedly at his glass of chilled white wine and endeavoured to focus his attention on the conversation that continued around him.

Just when he'd resigned himself to the totally unpalatable but quite likely possibility that she'd decided to stand him up at the last minute, he saw her. Emily had assured him that the dress she'd helped Sophie pick was *exquisite*. Now, as Dominic's starved gaze crossed the distance of the marble floor that separated them, he saw with satisfaction that his friend had been quite right.

Sophie was standing next to a liveried steward, her lovely face in profile, the black full-length silk halter dress clung devotedly to her slender curves, showcasing her creamy shoulders and revealing quite the most tantalising glimpse of cleavage that he could imagine. Dominic's wasn't the only admiring glance that was drawn Sophie's way.

Even as he politely excused himself from the company he'd been with he sensed his blood infused with a building and eager excitement as he approached her, quietly stunned by the most intense reaction to a woman he'd experienced in a very long time. It merely illustrated to Dominic how much he'd anticipated seeing her again, and how impatient he'd grown in the interim, when he couldn't see her. Normally having no trouble whatsoever sleeping at night, no matter what had gone on during the day, for the past five nights, since he'd dropped Sophie home on Saturday, he had barely been able to sleep at all. Thoughts of the girl he'd spent two extremely passionate nights with had tortured him mercilessly, leaving his body aching and hungry, as though he were under the spell of some erotic love potion. He needed her in his bed *tonight*. There'd be no nonsense about her having to go home. He simply wouldn't hear of it.

'Mr Van Straten,' the steward said formally, 'I was just about to bring Miss Dalton over to you.'

'Thank you.'

Waiting until the man had left their side, Dominic delved deep into Sophie's startled cornflower-blue eyes with restless need, trying to gratify all the longing of the past five days in her absence.

'I'm sorry I'm late…staff meeting ran on a bit, and I couldn't get away. Start of the new financial year and all…that.' Her words petered out as she realised she was babbling, and that Dominic's lips remained worryingly unsmiling.

Was he furious with her for being late? Sophie fretted,

glancing round at the other impeccably attired guests. There hadn't been a lot she could do when she'd received the note at the end of class yesterday afternoon, advising her of the meeting. 'All staff are expected to attend', it had stated clearly, and Sophie hadn't wanted to say she was going to an important function and then have to explain why. The gossip regarding her lift on Friday had died down a little, but not as much as Sophie would have liked.

Now, as her gaze swung nervously back to Dominic's, her heart nearly stalled when she saw the way his blazing emerald eyes were devouring her. Inside her lovely silk dress her body tightened and tingled in helpless response. The crowd in the room melted away, because only one person demanded all her focus and attention...Dominic. She'd been secretly longing to see him again, but the awesome reality of the man's physical presence was almost too much to bear. His hard, fit body did things for that expensive tuxedo that would make the tailor who'd designed it weep for joy.

'You are here now, and that is all that matters.'

Still unsmiling, he put his hand beneath Sophie's elbow and was just about to lead her back into the glittering anteroom when the master of ceremonies announced that dinner was about to be served—could all guests please make their way into the dining room?

Half an hour later, seated at the top table with her handsome escort, dinner under way, Sophie glanced around at the sea of dignitaries and their partners, then back to Dominic. His profile, with its crown of bright hair, reminded her beguilingly of a beautiful Greek god—the kind paid homage to in sculptures. A little stab of pleasure jolted through her stomach.

Everybody wanted to talk to him, it seemed. And, although Sophie secretly yearned to have him to herself, she knew that in this glittering arena of worthies and VIPs Dominic Van Straten was 'king' and she was a mere admirer—along with all the other eager admirers who waited their turn to be noticed by him.

Reaching for her glass, Sophie took a too-hurried sip of wine and promptly spilled some down the front of her dress—the wildly expensive designer gown that Emily Cathcart had insisted that Dominic was only too delighted to pay for.

As she tried in vain to brush the spreading stain away, Dominic glanced down at her side and touched his hand to her thigh. For a long moment the press of his hand against her flesh—albeit beneath the sensuous silk of her gown—felt as if it had scorched Sophie, and she caught the hot flare of desire in his gaze and barely knew how to breathe.

'I'd better go and find a bathroom.' Already pushing back her chair, and feeling overwhelmingly self-conscious as several interested pairs of eyes at their table turned her way, she was astonished to see Dominic rise to his feet, too.

'Excuse us,' he announced to no one in particular, 'but I think my companion is in need of a little help.'

'You don't have to—'

'I very much *do* have to,' Dominic assured her in a vehement whisper as he deliberately guided her away from the tables and out of the palatial dining room.

Without a word, Sophie quickened her pace to keep up with his commanding stride, following him down thickly carpeted silent corridors to a door marked 'Powder Room'. As she turned to thank him for his help, Sophie's blue eyes grew round with shock when he opened the door behind her, gave her a gentle shove inside, then promptly joined her. Inside the scented room, with its gleaming mirrors and padded chairs, the purely naked lust reflected in Dominic's mesmerising gaze backed Sophie nervously up against a wall. Feeling her heart beat so fast she was certain that at any moment now she would fall to the ground in a faint, she saw his hand reach out to slide around her neck, and she moved inexorably towards him as though in a dream she had absolutely no control over.

'You—you really shouldn't be in here, you know. This is the— This is the—' But her words were drowningly cut off by Dominic's hard, hot mouth on hers, capturing her breath with a soul-shattering kiss and smashing every last bit of resistance Sophie might own to dust. Her body yielded like a rag doll's as he hauled her desperately against his own implacable contours of finely honed muscle and bone. And she had no thought to stop him when his hand slid down and deliberately palmed her breast beneath her silk gown, his thumb and finger coaxing the already aroused tip into pure burning sensation.

'Did I tell you how amazing you look in that dress?' Dominic breathed against the side of her bare neck, his heat skimming across her flesh like naked blue flame.

Before Sophie could even think to form an answer, he stole another voracious kiss, leaving her lips swollen and tingling and her head swimming, then stepped away and raked his fingers agitatedly through his precision-cut blond hair.

Dominic was in no doubt she was temptation personified. In that sexy, yet undoubtedly classy black silk dress, so perfectly chosen by his friend, Sophie Dalton was a *siren*, a mythical creature of dreams and wild imagination come to life to taunt him. The more he saw her, the *more* Dominic wanted her. He might have spent most of the evening so far talking to all and sundry apart from Sophie, but the mere fact that she'd been sitting just a few inches away from him had made his blood sing and his thoughts race. So much so that he was certain any comments he'd been making had hardly made any sense at all.

The idea that had formed and started to take shape back at the hotel in Suffolk was slowly but surely becoming more real—not to mention more *urgent*. It was playing on his mind like a symphony, the sound of which refused to leave him morning, noon or night. And Dominic fully intended to make it into the reality he desired.

'I want you to come back home with me this evening. I have something I want to discuss with you.'

Furrowing her brow, Sophie stepped away from the wall and smoothed her hands down the front of her dress. The damp stain from the spilled wine was not to be seen. It wouldn't have surprised her if the heat from their bodies—hers and Dominic's—had all but scorched it dry.

'What do you want to talk to me about?' She tried to scan her mind for reasons, but her teeming brain wouldn't readily yield anything very much. She was still feeling dazed from the passionate little scene she had been an unexpected player in just now.

'Now is not the time or the place,' he said in a clipped voice, his hand straightening his jacket sleeve as he assumed his previous cloak of formality.

How did he do that? Sophie wondered in awe. How could he be full of fire and passion one minute, then in the next appear so cool and remote—as though he couldn't possibly be acquainted with something so primeval as lust, at all? It made her want to go over to him, strip his jacket and shirt from his back and ruffle him up a little, with the provocation of her body.

'It will be late when we leave here, won't it? I want to get up early in the morning, to go for a swim, so I'll probably just go straight home afterwards, if you don't mind.'

Dominic could hardly believe she was turning down yet another invitation of his. Good God! What was this woman trying to do to him? Never before in the whole of his romantic history with women had Dominic been made to wait for *anything*. Let alone a stubborn slip of a girl who resisted every single request he put her way! He was seriously beginning to wonder if his own hardly insignificant attractions were no longer to be relied upon. Yet he knew he hadn't imagined her fierce response to his lovemaking, and so he calculated without conceit that any resistance in other departments must be purely to whet his appetite—to make his desire all the keener. *He could have told her that she already had him driven so crazy with lust that she needn't bother trying to whet his appetite with game-playing.* But first he had to persuade her to come home with him.

'I have a swimming pool in my house, as well as a selection of costumes available for my guests. You can swim there to your heart's content and you will not be disturbed by other members of the public.'

He turned towards the door, as though the matter were at an end, and Sophie took immediate umbrage at the way he so casually assumed she would do what *he* wanted her to do. When she'd been with Stuart, Sophie had regularly and idiotically relinquished some of her own needs in deference to meeting the needs of her boyfriend. *Look how he'd repaid her.* She had no intention of behaving in such a submissive way again...with *anyone*.

'I don't want to swim at your house, Dominic! I want to go home and go to my own sports centre, like I usually do on a Saturday morning!'

At her unexpected outburst he turned to regard her, with a frosty look in his green-eyed stare.

'You are such a creature of habit that you can't break an insignificant arrangement to be with me?'

'It may appear ''insignificant'' to you, but it's not to me! I am sure you would not break an appointment that meant a lot to you in preference to being with me, would you?'

Her chest heaving in indignation, Sophie felt her annoyance quickly replaced by something far more disconcerting to her peace of mind when one corner of Dominic's mouth quirked upwards into a provocative little half-smile.

'Haven't I already demonstrated how much I want to be with you, Sophie? I *could* go home after this, and work. I'm flying to Geneva on Sunday for five days. The deal I'm hoping to close there will mean employment for several hundred nationals. I hope to win it over a rival who would greedily cost-cut efficiency and good labour in order to make more money. Negotiations will be complex and difficult. The more preparation I do the better. That is something ''important'' to me—yet I would rather spend the time with you. I really do not know how else I may convince you of my sincerity in this wish.'

Put like that, how *could* Sophie refuse? She felt slightly shame-faced. It wasn't as though it was *really* any contest—swimming at the sports centre pool or going home with Dominic. It was just that the more time she spent with this man, the harder she knew it was going to be when they had to part. Dominic wasn't *serious* about her. She'd be a fool to believe that for even a second. Sooner or later this…this hot sexual thing they had going on between them would fizzle out, and he would go on to the next obliging pretty female who would gladly try and fulfil his every whim.

A soft, resigned sigh escaped her. 'If it's that important to you, I'll come home with you, Dominic. But I don't have any spare clothes with me for tomorrow. Could we drop off at my place on the way home to get some?'

'No problem.'

He had assumed the veneer of formality again, and Sophie experienced a sudden fervent wish that they could go home together right now, instead of returning to that 'stiff' formal gathering in the dining room. Anything to see the compelling light of attraction dancing in his eyes again when he looked at her.

'Oh, and…Dominic?'

'What is it?'

'Thank you for the beautiful dress.'

'It is my pleasure, Sophie…believe me.'

Sophie hadn't thought about the Press being at the banquet, but soon after Dominic had presented the award to a smiling recipient, and had his picture taken with the man, a gaggle of photographers descended on their table, snapping away at Dominic as though he were some kind of movie star.

When he insisted on pulling her to his side, whispering provocatively against her ear, for her hearing alone,

'Smile as though you are crazy about me,' Sophie found the smile frozen on her face.

She wished she were anywhere but where she was. She had always hated being the centre of attention. Which was another reason why weddings and the thought of being a bride filled her with horror. She didn't stop hyperventilating until they were finally in the car alone, with Louis driving.

After grabbing some clothes for tomorrow from her maisonette, and having been driven back to Dominic's lovely house in Mayfair, Sophie suddenly felt as if she could drop with tiredness. It had been a hectic, demanding day, and it wasn't over yet.

Settling herself in one of the sumptuous white couches that dotted the room, Sophie picked up a stunning velvet cushion and hugged it defensively to her middle. Dominic had told her again on the way home that he had something important to discuss with her, and right now her heart was all but leaping out of her chest at the thought of what it could be.

'Brandy?' he asked over his shoulder as he crossed the room to the walnut display case.

'Not for me, thanks. I'm so tired that if I drink any more alcohol you're going to have to carry me up to bed.'

Her lips froze as the words left her mouth. She couldn't believe she'd said such an unguarded thing!

Dominic turned to glance at her with a highly speculative and amused gleam in his unsettling gaze.

'Whether you have a drink or not, Sophie, the idea holds undoubted appeal for me as I am sure you are only too aware!'

Mutely, she pursed her lips. When he joined her just moments later on the couch, removing his exquisite jacket, throwing off his tie and loosening his shirt collar, the blood in Sophie's veins started to thrum with helpless desire. *Want* curled deep into her vitals, almost making her whimper out loud, and the sensual foray of his inviting cologne mingling with the intoxicating heat from his body merely helped exacerbate that desire.

'What was it you wanted to talk to me about?' she forced herself to ask through suddenly dry lips.

'I have had an idea.'

'Oh?'

Clutching the cushion to her middle even tighter, Sophie realised she was holding herself so stiffly that a pain had started between her shoulderblades. With a huge effort, she willed herself to try and relax.

'What do you mean, exactly?'

Dominic took a sip of his brandy before continuing, his expression serious. It drew Sophie's powerless gaze to the hard, clean lines of his implacable jaw, and a little frisson of awareness ran down her spine.

'A man in my position has many responsibilities, Sophie. Great wealth brings with it great responsibility. Contrary to what many people might think, I cannot just simply sit back and let the people who work for me take care of everything. I am actively involved in most of the decision-making that goes on around me. No doubt you think that makes me quite the control freak, but it is an action that is born out of great desire to do things well. I cannot stand mediocrity in any way. Whatever one does in life, one should do it to the very best of their ability. Don't you agree?'

Knowing the monumental desire she had herself, to be an inspiring and enthusiastic teacher and never to rest on her laurels as far as her pupils were concerned, Sophie gave a little nod.

'Lately, I have come to the conclusion that my particular path in life should not always be travelled alone. I am fast coming round to the idea that it would be much assisted by having someone in my life to share it with me. That is where *you* come in, Sophie.'

'Me?' Her throat was as parched as gravel. *Where was this leading?* she speculated in fright.

'Yes, you.'

Putting down his brandy glass on the coffee-table in front of him, Dominic adjusted his body so that he was facing her. As his compelling green eyes briefly skimmed the low-cut front of Sophie's dress, she barely knew where to look, she was so undone.

'I am tired of the short, unsatisfactory associations that have lately been my experience. I'm asking you to come and live with me, Sophie, and be my mistress.'

Momentarily struck dumb, Sophie stared. *Were live-in lovers still called 'mistresses' these days?* Her racing mind tried to assimilate her feelings on the matter. Never in a million years could she have contemplated someone like Dominic asking her such a thing! Did he really think that she would seriously consider such a position in his life?

'You mean be like a…a kept woman?'

Dominic threw her an impatient look. 'Is it so impossible for you to visualise yourself being looked after by me?'

'I don't want to be looked after by any man! I have a career I love, a home of my own. Why would I give that up?'

She is impossible! Dominic thought furiously. She had pricked his ego a thousand times since they had met, and short of begging her to take the role he so longed for her to take— His thoughts broke off, because for a moment they slammed against a brick wall.

'Have you not considered the fact that I am offering you the kind of opportunity a lot of young women your age would jump at? Think about it, Sophie. You would not want for anything. We could travel together. You would see parts of the world you have never seen before, and everywhere we go we would travel and stay in luxury and style. Does that sound like something abhorrent to you?'

He really didn't get her at all, Sophie realised disconsolately. *He thought she could be bought with his money and his billion-dollar lifestyle.* The so-called opportunity he was offering was a million miles away from what her secret heart truly longed for.

Then she was stricken by another, even more disconsolate thought.

'Is this some kind of a joke, Dominic?' Hurt at the idea of being strung along by him for some kind of sick amusement, she felt heartfelt pain wend through her bloodstream. It *had* to be a joke. Billionaires didn't proposition ordinary little primary-school teachers every day. The blood seemed to drain from his face.

'It is most definitely *not* a joke, Sophie. I have thought very carefully about this and I am perfectly serious.'

'It would be impossible!'

Rising to her feet, Sophie let the velvet cushion fall unheeded back onto the couch as she moved away from it, clasping her arms protectively across her chest as she turned back to face Dominic.

'Why?' His expression was stony, and hardly inspired confidence.

'Because you can't have thought about it carefully enough! We are poles apart, Dominic, can't you see that? What use would someone like me be to you? Take this evening. I was like a fish out of water in that imposing place! I was tongue-tied and self-conscious, and I absolutely hated having my picture taken by the Press! I'm a very private person…not someone who remotely seeks attention. The last thing I need is to be ''mistress'' to someone who is the total opposite of that!'

'I do not seek attention!'

'No, but because of who you are, your wealth and your business acumen, you can't help but command it. Be honest, Dominic. You don't really need someone like me as a mistress. Besides, I'm sure you know a lot more suitable candidates.'

She didn't say that if he had included a little more emotion or *feeling* in his proposition it would have perhaps been more palatable—even if she still wouldn't seriously have considered it. But Sophie wasn't a fool, and she didn't suspect for even a second that Dominic would have any feelings of affection for her at all. The only thing the two of them had going between them was a sexual passion so sizzling that they could start a fire just by gazing at each other. It would hardly make up for all the other glaring opposites in their relationship. And, besides all that, Sophie didn't *want* to be any man's mistress. Her independence was important.

She didn't want to entertain the fact that it was perhaps fear, as well as her belief that independence gave her more security than any man could, that stopped her from even considering the possibility of living with someone.

'I'm not considering other ''candidates'' for the position. Think about it, Sophie. You need never work or *want* for anything as long as you are with me. All I ask in return is that you be there for me when I need you. Is that really so reprehensible to you?'

No doubt any other woman faced with the same extraordinary dilemma would be jumping for joy round about now—not feeling overwhelmingly sad that Dominic seemed to imagine that his vast wealth was the main inducement for Sophie agreeing to become his mistress. That thought *did* cause her grief. *Did the man never stop to think that a woman should love him for himself—for the man he was—before all else?*

'I did not say your proposal was reprehensible.'

When he said that all he'd ask in return would be for Sophie to 'be there for him whenever he needed her', she guessed he meant sexually, and also physically, if it was an occasion like the one at the Guildhall tonight, where a partner would come in handy. He clearly wasn't talking about her being there for him *emotionally*.

Feeling suddenly cold, Sophie walked back to the couch and sat down again. She picked up the cushion she had discarded and clutched it to her middle once more.

'I suppose I should be flattered that you considered asking me, but I don't want to be your mistress, Dominic. And I certainly don't want to give up work. I love my job. It may not provide all the amazing material benefits that your career does for you, but I love it just the same, and wouldn't swap it for the world.'

Once again Dominic was struck by her integrity. He could hardly believe that a woman so highly principled as Sophie existed. Her adamant insistence that she wanted to keep her job, no matter what inducements he might put her way, frankly stunned him. *But what to do about it?*

'What if I said you could keep your job and still live with me? If we could somehow work it so that you could make yourself available when I needed you, and not nec-

essarily interfere with the demands of your career…would that induce you to consider my proposal?'

Gazing back into his indomitably handsome face,
Sophie felt her heart constrict. She couldn't understand
why he wanted her to live with him. She really couldn't.
There must be dozens of women who'd jump at the
chance to be the mistress of Dominic Van Straten—and
women with far more suitable credentials than her own.
But, beneath her undoubtedly strong desire to be close
to this remote, enigmatic man, Sophie also knew a deep
desire to be loved. She'd barely expressed it, even to
herself, and especially not after her abortive attempt at
a relationship with the man who had betrayed her, yet
still she couldn't deny her profound longing for it. If she
moved in with Dominic it was highly doubtful that he
would ever love her. She might fulfil any number of
needs he had, but beyond that—not the one she craved
herself.

'Let's just go to bed, Dominic.'

Linking her hand in his, Sophie tugged a little. Just
because she couldn't agree to become his mistress, it
didn't mean that she had to deny her physical need to
be close to him.

When Dominic saw the strong evidence of that need
in her direct blue gaze, he was riveted by it. Never before had a woman had the power to unravel him so.

'Sophie…I fully intend to keep you preoccupied in
my bed for most of the night, but before we go upstairs
I must have your answer. Will you agree to come and
live with me?'

Her eyes never leaving his face, and feeling the threatening and surprising sting of tears behind her lids,
Sophie dropped her shoulders and sighed.

'I'm sorry, Dominic…but my answer has to be no.'

CHAPTER EIGHT

SOPHIE heard his deeply in-drawn breath with profound unease. Freeing his hand from hers with a cold glance that did not bode well for further conversation of any kind—let alone intimacy—he stood up, went to the door, and called for Andrews.

Convinced that he was calling for his manservant to fetch her coat, Sophie anxiously got to her feet and followed him to the door.

'It's late,' he said, his tone deliberately aloof. 'You can stay in one of the guest rooms for tonight, then in the morning you can enjoy your swim, as promised. Andrews will tell you where the pool is.'

So... He no longer wanted to spend the night with her because clearly her company had suddenly become repugnant to him.

'Don't be like this Dominic... Please.'

Swallowing hard over the pain that was cramping her throat, she tried to reach him with a smile. Even now, when he was clearly angry with her, she didn't know what to do with all the treacherous yearning for him that was pulsating through her. It consumed her like a fever and made every inch of her skin pine and ache for his touch. Her need was so powerful and relentless that it was like standing alone in a hurricane, knowing full well that she could be swept away any moment now—possibly into oblivion. Yet she didn't care.

'You want me to make love to you, yes? Yet you will not consent to being my mistress!'

Silently elated at the longing that was evident in her beautiful eyes, yet at the same time enraged that she had dismissed his proposal so easily, Dominic felt his pride silently warring with his staggering need to have her in his arms once again.

If he relented, he would no doubt spend another unforgettable night of breathless passion with her, and it would go some way to easing the incessant ache he had inside him for her touch. It was almost unbelievable to Dominic how great his desire for this woman was. But, as much as his body cried out for such vehement fulfilment, he would not relent to his need until Sophie consented to what he wanted. As a man who dealt ruthlessly with facts, he would use the very fact that Sophie was as passionately drawn to him as he was to her to gain the advantage he so desperately coveted.

And when he had gained that advantage, he would manipulate it to its natural conclusion…

'Go to bed, and when you cannot sleep because of the ache in your body that will not go away I want you to think about my offer, Sophie. Perhaps in the morning, in the new light of day, you may see all the advantages of such a union between us…and less of the disadvantages. Hmm?'

Knowing that his arrogance would normally infuriate her—even possibly make her walk out of his house and never come back—at that moment, gazing back into his deeply compelling eyes, Sophie could not make herself move. With her blood scorching so hotly through her veins that she could hardly think at all—never mind plan—she could not propel herself to do the thing that would probably serve her best.

'Dominic, I—'

'We will not discuss the matter any further tonight. There you are, Andrews,'

'Yes, sir?'

'I want you to show Miss Dalton to a guest room, and also give her directions to the pool for the morning. Goodnight, Sophie. Sleep well, won't you?'

And before Sophie could say anything else she was forced to bite back her words as Andrews politely indicated that she should follow him upstairs. As she reached the first landing, and glanced back down into the hall, Dominic was standing there: hands down by his sides, staring up at her with a provoking little smile that made her want to run to him and beg him to take her to bed. Aghast at how weak-willed she was around this man, Sophie glanced quickly away and followed Andrews down the plushly carpeted corridor.

It was a miracle that she'd slept at all, in light of the way she and Dominic had parted. But now, as she did her laps in the gorgeous, ornate pool with its Romanesque friezes and blue and white mosaic tiles, the morning sun beaming in at her through the glass-domed ceiling, Sophie sensed the ache easing out of her body and an upsurge of energy replacing it.

She couldn't deny that the opportunity to swim totally uninterrupted like this was sheer joy. There were definitely some advantages about living in the lap of luxury she concluded, allowing herself a very wry smile.

Yet would she *seriously* entertain the idea of becoming Dominic's mistress and all that that entailed? She could converse with people on all types of subjects, yes—her teacher training had helped her enormously with that—and she could even make polite chit-chat, at a push—as long as it didn't go on too long. Yet she was no social hostess who could host fabulous dinner parties with ease, or spend her time going to haute couture fashion shows so that she would appear appropriately and fashionably dressed as the consort of a rich and important man.

She could just imagine what her parents would have to say about the whole thing! Her father, in his typically brusque no-nonsense manner, would immediately dismiss Dominic as 'no good'—else why wouldn't he ask Sophie to marry him and not just live with him?—and her mother would fret and worry that her daughter was going to get hurt.

As she reached the end of her lap Sophie paused in the deep end, treading water as she tried to marshal her thoughts. Now wasn't the time to be thinking about how other people would react should she relent to Dominic's proposition and move in with him. The question was, how did *she* feel about the whole idea?

Running her fingers across the smooth tiles, which surrounded the pool, Sophie briefly shut her eyes as a surge of powerful longing throbbed through her body. *She couldn't deny she wanted him.* But was sex a good enough reason to agree to what he desired? And if she did move in with him, became his mistress, wouldn't she be cheating herself out of the possibility of having someone really fall in love with her? *Yet how could she let someone else fall in love with her when her heart was already under threat of being stolen?*

'Good morning, Sophie.'

Her eyes flew open again at the sound of Dominic's voice. In shirtsleeves and suit trousers he walked alongside the pool towards her, his tall, commanding figure causing disconcerting butterflies to take up immediate residence in her stomach. Self-consciously she smoothed back her damp short hair.

'Morning.'

'I trust you slept well?'

There was no denying the barely veiled taunt in his voice, and heat spread between Sophie's thighs and travelled inexorably up to her breasts, the powerful extent of her passionate attraction to Dominic shocking her once again.

'It was a lovely comfortable bed, and, yes… I *did* sleep well.' Her answer was typically defiant…if unconvincing.

Unable to take his eyes off her, with her beautiful shoulders gleaming with wetness in the plain black costume she wore, and her gaze a sea of startling seductive blue, Dominic sensed a dizzying river of carnal longing rage forcefully through his veins. He had *not* slept so well…in spite of the comfort of his bed. It had not helped his case, either, when, driven to get up in the middle of the night, he'd taken a freezing cold shower to help ease his ardour. It had merely left him wide awake and aching with need. *Extremely* in need as he'd thought about Sophie, sleeping just a few doors down from his, in her room in the same corridor. *Had she given his proposal further and proper consideration?* he'd wondered?

Dominic absolutely despised the fact that she was keeping him on tenterhooks. He had never allowed himself to become this on edge about going into any potentially tricky negotiation or meeting. He had always had full confidence that his immaculate planning and consummate business acumen would win the day. He couldn't deny that he had taken his lead from his father and it had served him well.

'Never allow emotion to cloud your thinking,' he had

advised. 'Keep your head, don't be attached to the out-come and the desired result will flow to you with ease.'

But Dominic *was* attached to the outcome. He wanted Sophie to be his mistress. It would be true to say that he had become *obsessed* with the idea. Going out to dinner with his pick of beautiful women was no longer enough. He wanted just *one* beautiful woman in partic-ular to be his companion. He was tired of empty sexual encounters just to fulfil a basic need. Sophie was an en-chanting, engaging and *educated* woman. Someone he could converse with, discuss plans and ideas with, some-one he could spend time with and not be bored out of his mind in her company. Dominic wanted a longer-term companion to share the amazing fruits of his success. And the woman he wanted, the woman he *had* to have, was Sophie.

'So...' he said, crouching down beside her. 'You are ready to come out now and have some breakfast?'

At the answering growl in her stomach, Sophie si-lently acknowledged she was starving. She had hardly touched the food at the banquet last night, and after her vigorous swim she was even hungrier. Yet she was acutely self-conscious at the idea of climbing out of the pool and revealing herself in her costume. Even though it was plain black, its high cut on the legs and deep neckline barely left much to the imagination.

'I will get your towel.'

Without further preamble Dominic went to the nearby cane lounger where Sophie had left her towel and brought it to her. Standing at the edge of the tiled steps, he waited for her to come out.

Smoothing back her saturated hair with a nervous hand, Sophie started to walk up the steps towards him. Dominic stared, making no secret of the fact that he was enjoying the privilege, and Sophie's skin burned to have him look at her, because his glance was as potent and powerful as his very touch. When she got close, so close that she was intimately acquainted with the pupils of his eyes, Sophie held her breath, convinced that he was going to kiss her. When he didn't, but instead merely draped the towel around her shoulders and started to walk away, she bit back her bitter disappointment and shivered violently beneath the towel.

'We will breakfast in the conservatory,' he told her over his shoulder. 'Walk to the end of the corridor, turn left, then right, and you will find it. I'll wait for you there.'

Dressed in jeans and a plain white cotton shirt, her body still glowing warmly from her swim, Sophie found her way to the conservatory.. and the sight of Dominic lounging back in his chair reading a newspaper. Around him bustled a small olive-skinned woman dressed in a black dress and white apron—presumably his housekeeper—busily laying breakfast things on the table in front of him.

'Sophie…come and sit down. Maria will bring you some tea or coffee. What do you prefer?'

'Tea, please,' Sophie replied, taken aback when Dominic stood up and pulled out a chair for her, then waited until she was seated before resuming his own seat.

'And to eat? Do you like the "full English breakfast," or are you one of those abstemious women who either don't eat at all or eat only fruit in the morning?'

Surprised at his light banter, Sophie couldn't help but grin. 'I *definitely* couldn't survive the morning on just fruit, so I would very much like the full English, if that's all right? The only time I ever get a cooked breakfast is if I go home to my mum's, so it will be a treat.'

Having grown up with a mother who had spent her days fundraising and social climbing, Dominic had *never* experienced anything so homely as having a breakfast cooked by his own mother. A brief flare of envy surfaced as he regarded Sophie's pretty, animated face, and he caught himself wondering if she would do the same for her own children. His envy was quickly replaced by a moment of deep and profound reflection on the topic. Then, realising that Maria hovered at his side waiting for his instruction, he asked his housekeeper for two cooked breakfasts and a large pot of tea. As she bustled away, he levelled his interested gaze back to Sophie.

'Do you see your parents often?' he asked conversationally.

'About two or three times a month, at most. I'm afraid I *do* tend to get rather caught up in my work. When I'm not at school, teaching, I'm either studying or attending courses to try and improve myself. It doesn't leave much time for visiting anyone. My parents understand, though. They sacrificed a lot to send me to university.'

They sounded like good people. Dominic's interest deepened. 'What does your father do?' he asked her.

'He's a builder. He works too hard, though, and he's getting on a bit. I do worry that he overreaches himself a bit too much physically. Only last month he hurt his back and was off for two weeks.' The memory jolted Sophie into a regretful reverie. Her dad was back at work now, but she should go and see him soon—make sure for herself that he was doing all right. Realising that Dominic was studying her intently, Sophie reached for the perfectly folded white linen napkin in front of her, shook it out and laid it carefully on her lap.

'What does *your* father do?' she asked quietly.

'He's a businessman. Officially retired, but still with his fingers in a lot of different pies.' Dominic's smile was rueful, and a little twinge of pleasure flared in Sophie's stomach.

'And what about your mother?' she ventured.

He shrugged, and a veil seemed to come down over his eyes. 'She keeps herself busy travelling and doing a lot of things for charity.'

'And do you get to see her very much?'

The last time had been almost a year ago, and that had been only briefly when she had made a flying visit to his office in London. 'No. Not really.'

'Oh.'

Sophie didn't know what else to say. Whether his comment signalled that he regretted that fact, or simply didn't care one way or the other, she couldn't have said. But the absent look on his face tugged at her heartstrings somehow.

'I'm sure it's a very tough job being a parent. I take my hat off to those hardy individuals brave enough to try. When I think of the energy and demands of my class of five-year-olds, I can almost feel my hair turning grey at the thought!'

'But eventually…you would like children of your own?'

Dominic's question hung poised in the air, as threatening to Sophie's sense of safety as if she stood with her toes out over the edge of a cliff. She shifted uncomfortably.

'Not for ages yet. I'd have to be married first, and I haven't found anyone who—' She turned crimson as the words spilled out, and suddenly stopped as she realised what she was saying.

Beneath his light tan, Dominic's skin appeared momentarily flushed, and she knew the topic of becoming his mistress, as he had proposed, had been bubbling all the while beneath the surface of their ordinary conversation, and was about to come up again.

'I have come up with an idea that I would like you to consider.'

Frowning at this new development, Sophie linked her hands together in her lap and sat waiting.

'What idea is that?'

'A trial period of six months' duration. We will live together for six months, and if at the end of that period you find that the arrangement is not to your liking, for whatever reason, you can move out again and I will not pressurise you into staying. Does that idea perhaps hold more appeal than tying yourself to me indefinitely?'

Her heart thudding heavily in her chest, Sophie stared. 'Why do you want me to live with you at all? Why can't we just see each other like other couples do?'

Because with his schedule and her schedule Dominic thought they would barely get to see each other at all. At least if Sophie lived with him, there would be times when he could press her into travelling abroad with him on meetings and spur-of-the moment trips, etc. He was certain that once she got a taste of the kind of world-class travel that was the norm for Dominic she wouldn't object too loudly about travelling with him. And he might be able to persuade her that her career perhaps wasn't as important as she thought it was after all.

'Because that's not what I want. I want you to move in, or I will hardly get to see you at all. I have this big beautiful house and lots of room. It shouldn't be too much of a hardship for you.'

'So you have this idea that you're somehow rescuing

me from my lowly lifestyle? You think perhaps that I should be very grateful that you're making me this once-in-a-lifetime offer?'

For a moment Sophie was furious at his implication that what he was offering was such a fabulous inducement that she should immediately forget everything she'd worked so hard to achieve for herself and simply just move in with him and let herself be kept! Okay, she relented silently. It *was* a fabulous inducement, and plenty of other women might have jumped at the chance to be the live-in lover of a gorgeous rich billionaire like Dominic, but Sophie *wasn't* one of those women. As much as her feelings for him had grown, she would not relinquish her life totally for him.

'I do not understand why you are being so stubborn. Anyone would think I was offering you something despicable!'

'You don't understand because you don't really know me at all, Dominic! I love my work—I even love my little house—even though it could probably fit into your place ten times over! They both mean a lot to me.'

Sighing with undisguised exasperation, Dominic pushed his fingers through his hair. 'What if we agree that you could keep your little house, and your job, and still move in with me? What would you say to that, Sophie?'

'And if I agreed?' Her mouth going dry at the very idea of moving in with Dominic and sharing his fabulous lifestyle, Sophie nervously skimmed her tongue over her top lip. 'What…what would you expect of me, Dominic?'

He answered without flinching, direct and to the point. 'I would expect you to be my companion and my lover…of course. What else did you think I would expect, Sophie?'

Feeling hot at his undoubted implication that being his lover would be the most important part of all, Sophie felt her thoughts scatter wildly, like leaves swept up in a gust then blown away again.

'If I were to…to consider this new proposal…I want it to be understood that I won't give up my career. I'll live with you, and assume the role you want me to, but only if it is understood that I come and go as I please. I'm used to my independence and I won't consider anything less. I *couldn't*.'

Feeling hugely relieved and quietly elated, Dominic allowed his deceptively calm expression to give very little away as Sophie sat there looking back at him. He would give way on her desire to keep her job, he was thinking, but he would not want her to be too independent. When she realised that he was willing to give her everything her heart desired, she would soon come to accept that in effect Dominic was the boss, and that naturally *his* needs were the ones that would take precedence. Besides, if she were going to be his mistress he would want her beside him on his travels round the globe. Sometimes he was gone for weeks at a time, and there was no way that he would be leaving Sophie once she'd agreed to live with him—otherwise what would be the point of going through with the arrangement at all?

'We have an agreement, then?'

Reaching for her hand, he twined it in his own, his smooth fingers weaving through hers with a definitely possessive air.

Telling herself that she had well and truly taken complete and utter leave of her senses for even considering

Dominic's proposal—especially in light of the fact she hadn't exactly even been considering another relationship for a long, long time—Sophie could barely articulate a reply.

'I—I would like some time to take all this in before I move in. Do you agree?'

'How much time?'

'A week…maybe two?' She shrugged, indecision temporarily freezing her brain.

'I will give you seven days, then this time next week I will arrange for your things to be moved here.'

'And what about your family and friends, Dominic? Will you tell them about me?'

He avoided answering by turning the question around. 'Will you tell *your* parents?'

'There wouldn't be any point. Not when—not when it's not even a proper relationship.' Her expression was pained, and Dominic squeezed her fingers hard with his own.

'You are wrong! Of course it will be a proper relationship. Your parents will have no cause for concern. How could they, when I will look after you and you will want for nothing? I am merely suggesting the six months' trial period so that you do not feel as though I have trapped you into this arrangement. You can tell whoever you choose about it.'

'So you will tell your parents, too?' Sophie asked him, wide-eyed.

Yes, he would tell them. But he didn't expect them to jump for joy. Not when his mother found out that his new paramour was a simple primary school teacher, with working-class parents, and not the daughter of wealthy or even professional people. His mother expected her son to have relationships, of course, but she was very much a snob at heart, when all was said and done, and only expected the best for her one and only son. His father might frown and ask him if he could not have done better, but he would not disturb him half as much as his mother. Especially when she *met* Sophie. She was unlike any other girl Dominic had ever dated, neither a social climber nor a gold digger, and that, of course— apart from the hot sexual attraction that sizzled between them—was another reason for her appeal.

'Of course.'

Sophie didn't dare speculate if Dominic's parents would like her, should they ever meet. She had enough trouble focusing on the fact that she had agreed to become Dominic's mistress and—even more pertinent— what living with Dominic Van Straten was going to be like!

Back at work on Monday, it really only hit Sophie then—what she was proposing to go through with and the effect it would no doubt have on her life.

She'd been fully expecting to receive a phone call from Dominic in Geneva, where he had flown yesterday, to tell her he had thought over the matter some more and he was sorry but he'd made a terrible mistake. When she'd received no such communication Sophie had gone about the rest of her weekend in a complete daze, nervously reminding herself that she needed to pack some things ready for moving in with him in only a few short days' time. She'd also had a postcard from Diana in Cyprus, where she was on honeymoon, and the sight of her friend's familiar handwriting had made Sophie's stomach seesaw, as if she'd just polished off a glass of neat vodka before breakfast.

Diana would hardly be able to believe it! Away for

just a fortnight, only to return and find out that her best friend was moving in with her boss! And after they had clearly disliked each other intensely on sight!

'Good weekend, Sophie?' Barbara Budd asked slyly as she poured herself a coffee from the machine in the book-laden staffroom.

Pretending to concentrate on the staff bulletin she was reading on the board, Sophie shrugged lightly. 'Okay. How about you?'

'Nothing too exciting. Seen anything of your rich boy-friend lately?'

Feeling dizzying heat pulse through her body at the question, Sophie spun round. 'What are you talking about?' Studying the other woman uneasily, she felt a keen stab of dislike at the unconstrained curiosity in her eyes.

'You know very well what I'm talking about, Sophie. The one who owns the Rolls Royce. I wouldn't let him go in a hurry, if I were you. I'd jump at the chance to say goodbye to this place!'

It was well known by the other members of staff that Barbara hadn't chosen teaching as a vocation. She hadn't got the grades she'd wanted to study as a lawyer, so teaching was a poor second-best in her eyes. Sophie couldn't help but feel sorry for the class of eight-year-olds she taught.

'I'd really prefer it if you just minded your own business, Barbara, if you want to know the truth! My private life is nothing to do with you.'

'Pardon me for breathing, I'm sure.'

Tossing her head, the other woman picked up her vo-luminous handbag and marched out of the room as though she were the Queen of Sheba herself making an exit. Feeling her shoulders droop with a mixture of relief and defeat, Sophie collected her things together and made her way slowly to her classroom. At least that was one arena where she didn't feel so mixed up and afraid.

CHAPTER NINE

DOMINIC had rung Sophie to ask that she come with Louis to the airport to meet him. Almost a whole week had gone by since he'd left for Geneva, and every day that passed Sophie had surprisingly found herself missing him more. Stunned by such a heartfelt reaction, she barely knew what to do with all the tumultuous feelings that were racing around inside her. She carried his absence around with her as though she were bereaved, and even doing the simplest of tasks seemed to require an almost monumental effort of concentration. All she could think about was Dominic.

Not liking the idea that she'd become obsessed with the man, she'd irritably tried to shake off her morose mood. She'd even gone out a couple of evenings in succession for a drink with friends, determined to demonstrate to herself that she was definitely not one of those silly women who could only survive if they had a man in their life. It hadn't worked. All she could do when she got home again was play some unashamedly romantic CD and moon around the house as though some mysterious sickness had descended upon her.

Now, as she paced the VIP lounge at Heathrow, too restless to even pick up a magazine and read it, Sophie glanced nervously down at the lovely coat that Dominic had insisted she keep. It made her secretly marvel at how one thing could lead to another and take you down a very different path from the one you'd been intent on travelling. From a girl who'd wondered if she'd ever have a relationship again because she'd become so commitment shy to contemplating moving in with a man she'd only just met was a pretty big detour in a person's life. She'd even taken particular care with her make-up this evening, because she wanted to look especially nice for Dominic, and Louis had kindly commented on how well she looked when he'd come to pick her up.

'Sophie.'

A little bolt of heat shot through her at the unexpected sound of that voice. Slowly she turned, her heart leaping with unconstrained joy at the sight of him with a stylish raincoat thrown over his dark suit, his blond hair a little mussed and a suggestion of darkness beneath his amazing eyes that immediately concerned her. All it took was just one little glance to make Sophie lose her centre of gravity. Suddenly finding herself completely at a loss for words, she willed her feet to move forward, but remained where she stood as Dominic disconcertingly smiled and travelled towards her instead.

The long meeting-filled days of the past week had somehow taken more out of him than Dominic liked. He'd had to fight for his position long and hard, coming up against stiff opposition from his rivals and having to revise plans, assessments and financial projections deep into the night every night he was there, to come up with a viable and realistic package that would win him the deal. His main desire that several Swiss nationals would win gainful employment through his efforts had overridden his usual number-one need to make a substantial profit. *The deal had been won.*

Elated, but weary, Dominic had flown home with only one aim in mind to ease the tension and fatigue that had accumulated over the past few days. *Sophie.* He was desperate to see her, to make certain that she knew he fully intended her to keep to their arrangement and move in with him either the following day or the day after that. He'd allowed her her seven days to take it all in, and he didn't want to wait any longer.

He'd made up his mind that he would make her remember how good they were together tonight in bed. The thought of that had sustained him throughout the flight, and now it was all he could think about. As his gaze settled on her small, slender figure, Dominic was gratified to see that she was wearing the coat he'd bought her, and he couldn't suppress a rush of excitement that chased his previous tiredness away and made him feel amazingly and insatiably *alive*.

'How are you?' he asked her, unable to prevent the definite traces of need and emotion straining his voice.

'I'm fine.' Smiling up at him, Sophie kept her hands down by her sides, nervous and unsure how to greet him even though instinct dictated that she fling her arms around him and kiss him.

But he looked almost too untouchable for her to concede to such unconstrained emotion in public. Dominic was exactly what he appeared: a perfectly groomed and handsome businessman, successful and wealthy beyond measure, from the tips of his shoes to the top of his gilded head. He wasn't just Sophie's boyfriend, returning home from a trip abroad. When this man said 'jump' people automatically responded with 'How high?' That put the matter of his homecoming into an entirely different perspective for Sophie.

For a long moment she was struck by how sheer outrageous fortune had manoeuvred her into the same amazing sphere as this man. *How could a relationship between two people from such diametrically opposite circumstances possibly work?* she thought soberingly. It was about time she woke up out of the dream she'd been in and started to get real.

'Don't I get a welcome-home kiss?' Dominic goaded softly, his honeyed voice commanding her attention.

Her stomach churning with nerves, knowing she would have to talk to him about this forthcoming arrangement of theirs again, Sophie stood on tiptoe and planted a deliberately informal kiss on his cheek. A mere peck.

Straight away, Dominic scowled. 'If that kiss was any true indication of how much you've missed me, then I am sorry indeed.'

'You look tired,' Sophie replied, latching on to the first excuse she could think of to explain her behaviour.

'But not so tired that I do not have the strength to show my woman that I have been thinking of her while I have been away...hmm?'

His lips descended on hers before Sophie could turn her head away. They were hungry and warm and sent fire rippling through her veins like the after-effects of cognac. Because she simply couldn't help it, she opened her mouth and drank the taste of him in, her heart pounding so hard inside her chest that she needed to hold onto Dominic until the dizziness that had overtaken her passed.

When he lifted his head to look down at her, he stroked her chin with the pad of his thumb and smiled. 'Perhaps you *did* miss me a little...huh?'

'How—how did your work go?' Standing back from him a little, Sophie smoothed her slightly trembling hand down her coat.

'Very satisfactory, since you ask. But I don't want to discuss work with you now, Sophie. All I want to do is go home, have a drink with you and go to bed. You will stay tonight, yes?'

He made it sound like such an easy and simple decision, and yet for Sophie it was as though she had to negotiate a path littered with landmines. The more she allowed herself to be intimate with Dominic, the harder it was going to be to walk away. Whether that would be six months down the road, at the end of their trial arrangement, or whether it would be tonight if Sophie confessed to him her doubts about their relationship—it made no difference. She'd missed him like crazy the whole time he'd been away, but maybe that was all the more reason for her to maintain a little sensible breathing distance between them? At least until she was certain she was doing the right thing.

'I'm sure you'd much rather just rest. It would probably be best if I just went home. I could come back tomorrow and see you, if you like?'

The distance she seemed to be trying to enforce between them both alarmed and infuriated Dominic. Had she been talking to someone about him while he was away? A friend, perhaps, who'd advised Sophie that moving in with him was a bad idea? If that was the case, then the sooner she moved in the better! Sophie would come to learn that people often had very preconceived ideas about wealthy and powerful men like him, and even friends would not necessarily always have her best interests at heart. Dominic wouldn't be surprised if some element of jealousy or envy had come into play during any 'friendly advice' she'd been given.

'Nonsense! I have waited all week to see you again, and now you tell me you want to go home tonight and will come back tomorrow? I won't hear of it. Of course you will stay with me tonight!'

His authoritarian stand immediately engendered resentment in Sophie. As much as she truly desired to be with him, she wouldn't be *ordered* to spend the night with him—as though she were some sort of powerless serf to his arrogant Lord of the Manor!

'Dominic... It might be second nature to you just to demand whatever you want and get it, and you might speak to other women that way, but in my book you ask first. This is the twenty-first century, remember? I come and I go at my own free will. I'm not your chattel!'

He sighed heavily and dragged his fingers impatiently through his hair, as though he found her indignation completely tedious.

'I cannot believe we are having an argument in the first few minutes of seeing each other! All right. I will concede that perhaps I should have asked you if you would like to spend the night. Well, I am asking you now, Sophie. Will you?'

All of a sudden Dominic was too weary to disguise the naked longing in his eyes. His guard down, all pretence fled in the wake of that powerful need. And on the receiving end of that revealing and earth-shattering look, Sophie sensed all her resistance rapidly melt away, like flotsam and jetsam carried off by the tide.

'If you're sure you're not too tired?'

'I am not an invalid, Sophie. I have only flown home from a business trip.' His gaze signalling his amusement at the very notion of being tired, Dominic took the liberty of tucking one of Sophie's tantalising curls gently behind her ear. 'I am quite happy to demonstrate my vigour to you as soon as we get home.'

Unable to do anything very much except blush scarlet, Sophie allowed him to take her hand and lead her out into the busy concourse that was Heathrow airport.

*   *   *

His bedroom was vast and stylish, the centrepiece a magnificently sumptuous draped four-poster bed. Sophie immediately felt lost inside such an imposing room, confronted as she was by the colossal differences in her own circumstances and Dominic's and wondering how not to feel intimidated.

But she soon had another challenge to contend with, when Dominic pulled off his tie, fixed her with a devastatingly possessive and sexy grin and then walked towards her with an altogether inflammatory glance that told her it wasn't their differences he was interested in right now. It was the one thing that they *definitely* had in common: their mutual *desire*.

'What are you doing?' she asked nervously, as Dominic's hands settled on her waist and with a forthright little pull brought her right up against his chest.

'What do you think I'm doing?' he asked, his hands caressing her back, then sliding down past the waistband of her jeans into her panties. 'I'm getting to know you all over again, Sophie Dalton.'

Even his voice, honey-rich and sensual, had the power to make Sophie lose all sense of reason. There was already such a primitive ache pulsating inside her that her very bones were restless with it. She forgot all about his status and wealth, and the fact that he lived in a house fit for royalty. When Sophie's guileless blue eyes met the glinting emerald of his, all they saw reflected back at her was a man—a very *human* and warm man who needed her touch just as much as she coveted his.

Raising her hand, she traced the outline of his near-perfect lips with her finger. A muscle throbbed in his cheek and he captured her hand, turned the palm towards him and kissed it. Just as Sophie went weak at his touch his mouth took ruthless possession of her lips and made her mindless with longing. Dominic Van Straten wasn't just a powerful and successful businessman. He was a man who knew how to kiss with the most devastating results. All his passion, all his *hunger* for intimacy and warmth, was contained in that all-consuming contact, and Sophie sensed a need in him that she hadn't been acquainted with before. An *emotional* need.

So he wasn't a remote 'island' after all? She seemed to have made the totally surprising discovery that his need to be loved was just as prevalent as any other human being's...just as prevalent as *her own*. Sophie kissed him back, barely conscious of the fact that they were moving in unison towards the bed, eagerly tearing at each other's clothes as though they couldn't wait for skin-to-skin contact.

In the lamplight Dominic's body exuded muscular strength in abundance, and he appeared like some mythical warrior of old—all golden hair and smooth, rippling biceps. He lay down and urged Sophie to straddle him. Persuasion was hardly necessary, because the primal need in her was swelling like a tide, and she couldn't wait so much as one minute more before joining her body with Dominic's. His length filled her with one smooth upward thrust and made her cry out with the pleasure of it.

Then suddenly he stilled, his hands resting on her thighs, as realisation stole into his hot gaze. 'Sophie, we need to use some protection. We can't take the risk of you falling pregnant.'

Even articulating the words, Dominic experienced the strongest and most surprising desire to make a baby with this woman. The awareness all but rocked his world off its axis. But even as he allowed himself the fantasy

Sophie was smiling down at him with her enchantingly shaped lips, her fingers sliding up his biceps and stroking them.

'You don't have to worry. I'm on the Pill. I take it for...because I have painful periods.'

Even though they were actually in the throes of making love, Sophie's cheeks heated with embarrassment at having to explain such an intimate reason for being on the Pill to Dominic. But this man was making her push at every emotional boundary she'd ever erected for herself, and she wasn't going to let embarrassment steal away the joy of being with him like this.

Hardly knowing whether to feel reassured or disappointed at the news, Dominic soon forgot his fantasy about making babies as Sophie slowly but very effectively rocked her slender hips against his, causing waves of volcanic pleasure to erupt inside him as his thrusts became deeper and more demanding. His hands covering her breasts, he stroked and played with the nipples that had hardened into dusky pink pebbles, enjoying her pleasure as much as his own. She started to exhale in breathy little gasps, calling out his name as he rocked into her with one more relentless thrust, and they both came apart in each other's arms. Sophie fell against him with her lips pressed into his chest, savouring every erotic musky scent that their entwined bodies exuded.

'Now, *that* is more like the homecoming I had in mind.' Chuckling softly, Dominic tangled his fingers into the short, silky strands of her hair, then slid both hands down the side of her face and lifted her head to make her look at him.

'We are not so different, you and I,' he told her, as he examined her flushed, aroused features. 'We are both passionate and fiery. A good combination, don't you think?'

'And you like passionate women? I mean, I'm sure you've known quite a few in your time, Dominic?' Feeling undeniably jealous at the thought, Sophie did not smile.

'A few...but never anyone like you, Sophie.'

'I've only had one proper boyfriend before you. Can you guess?'

'If you are asking me do I think your lack of experience shows, then, no. You are quite the femme fatale. Your sexy little body is enough to drive a sane man out of his wits with desire. Does that reassure you?'

Women would always look at Dominic and desire him. Sophie knew that. Whether she could handle it or not was another thing entirely. Until Stuart had betrayed her Sophie had never experienced the kind of jealousy that cut through a person's soul like a knife. For a while she'd despised the girl Stuart had spent the night with. But after a while she'd forced herself to let the hurt diminish and get on with her life. Nevertheless, she didn't particularly want to experience such pain again, if she could help it. *If she allowed herself to fall for Dominic unreservedly wasn't that the kind of pain she was signing up for? Only probably ten times worse...* A man as dynamic and charismatic as he was would always have many admirers. Sophie didn't doubt that a lot of them would be women.

'I wasn't fishing for compliments..really.'

She moved to lie by his side, staring up at the peach silk canopy that draped the sumptuous bed, feeling curiously vulnerable and afraid.

'I think the sooner we are together the better,' Dominic announced. He was a man of the world, but he did not particularly want to hear about Sophie's ex-boyfriend or wonder if she had been as easily aroused by him as she was with Dominic. 'You might like to spend some time thinking about where you would like me to take you for our first trip away,' he said, his fingers trailing gently down her cheek. 'I want us to go soon, so that we can spend a little time getting to know each other.'

Talking about trips away made Sophie's thoughts naturally gravitate to Diana. Her friend would be back at work for Dominic on Monday. Would she be surprised and pleased for her? Or would she be shocked that Sophie had taken such a U-turn and was contemplating a live-in relationship with Dominic when she'd so vehemently declared herself to be a man-free zone?

'Sophie?' Dominic coaxed softly, his glance concerned as she continued to stare up at the canopy without speaking.

'Soon, you say? Well, I just hope I can get time off school. If it coincides with the Easter break, then it will be fine. Otherwise, I might not be able to go.'

Unable to conceive that the school she worked for might make it difficult for Sophie to have time off, Dominic couldn't help but feel frustrated. If he had his way then Sophie would be handing in her notice, not pleading for permission to go on holiday!

'That is ridiculous!' He voiced his vexation out loud.

'No, Dominic,' Turning her head to study him, Sophie felt her heart leap helplessly at the sight of his fiercely handsome face. 'That's life. Even supply teachers are thin on the ground these days. And if I'm honest, I don't particularly want another teacher standing in for me while I'm away, anyway. The little ones get very attached to their teacher, and it takes them quite a while to adjust to someone new. I wouldn't want them to be upset in my absence.'

'Do you never take time off?' Dominic demanded, scowling.

'Of course! I get the school holidays off, like everyone else. But other than that I try and avoid it if I can. Like I said, the children—'

'Have you always been so stubbornly dedicated?'

Even as he posed the question Dominic knew he could hardly fault Sophie for a quality he meticulously adhered to himself, but part of him couldn't help feeling ridiculously jealous that she would put her class of five-year-olds before him.

'I've always wanted to teach. It was my dream career even as a little girl. Why wouldn't I be dedicated?'

'Did you never think that one day you might want a family of your own?'

Startled by the question, Sophie stared. 'I'm not saying that it's never crossed my mind, but there's still so much I want to do before—before that happens.'

Now it was his turn to glance up at the ceiling. Putting his arm behind his head, he sighed. 'I too have thought about having a family of my own one day. My work has really been my life, you know? But of course one must think of the future.'

Uncomfortable with the way the conversation was going, because it was clear to Sophie that when Dominic spoke of his desire for a family of his own he didn't mean with her, she bit back her hurt and forced a smile.

'Right now I would rather focus on the present…wouldn't you?'

'You echo my thoughts precisely. Clever girl!'

Before Sophie realised his intention he had moved, positioning himself above her, his strong thighs imprisoning her hips, and gazing down at her with a sexy little gleam in his eye that sent wild tingles of excitement racing up and down her body.

'Dominic…what are you doing?'

'I'm demonstrating my vigour, darling Sophie. Just like I promised you I would.'

Covering her surprised gasp with his mouth, coaxing her lips into a long, leisurely, extremely sexy kiss that felt like a dream she never wanted to wake up from, he commanded her full and devoted attention with exhilarating ease.

'I need to sit down.'

Finding one of Sophie's padded but threadbare armchairs close by, Diana sank down into it, her shocked face turning pale beneath her newly acquired Mediterranean tan.

'Let me get this straight. You're telling me that while I was away Dominic and you got it together and now he's asked you to move in with him? What the hell happened to make all this come about? The last impression I got from you before I left was that you couldn't *stand* him!'

Leaving the two steaming mugs of coffee she had made for them on the table, Sophie fingered a softly curling tendril at her ear and attempted a smile. 'I can hardly explain it myself, Diana, if you want to know the truth. It was just one of those crazy things that happen sometimes… Although I never thought it would happen to me.'

'He must be up to something.'

Her long scarlet nails curling into the faded material on the chair-arm, Diana appeared flustered and distracted. Sophie's heart thumped at her words, all her instincts immediately on alert.

'What do you mean, he must be up to something?'

'Be realistic, Soph! Here you are, an underpaid, over-worked, passably attractive primary school teacher, and there's Dominic—a mega-rich, mega-successful, drop-dead gorgeous hunk who reads the financial pages for relaxation and lives in just one of the most prestigious addresses in London! I mean, wake up and smell the coffee, Sophie! Yes, you're pretty, and I love you to bits, but you're no Catherine Zeta-Jones, darling!'

Her friend's words lambasted her like an unforgiving forest fire, treacherously flattening Sophie's self-esteem and pride. *Diana could be crass sometimes—but insensitive and cruel?* Right now, Sophie could have been looking at a stranger.

'Speak your mind, why don't you?' she said, hurt.

'For goodness' sake, Sophie! All he probably wants to do is sleep with you! He's obviously just teasing you with this "moving in" idea, to try and sweeten you up a little. He's found out you're not the kind of girl who sleeps around, and you can't be bought, so he's doing his damnedest to seduce you, that's all. As soon as he's got what he wants he'll drop you like a hot brick and move on to somebody else!'

'I've already slept with him, for your information.'

Feeling her throat tighten with pain at the realisation that Diana was clearly not the friend she'd thought she was, Sophie crossed her arms in front of her chest, her blue eyes glittering. 'And, as a matter of fact, he asked me to move in with him *after* we slept together!'

'I don't believe you!'

Pushing to her feet, Diana's gaze locked onto Sophie's with undisguised disdain.

'Why would he want to be with someone like you when he could have his pick of beautiful women? Do you know how many women ring him during a period of one week? You're just asking for trouble if you go through with this ridiculous arrangement, Sophie! He'll never be faithful to you! What reason would he have?'

CHAPTER TEN

HE'LL never be faithful to you...what reason would he have? The question caused her insurmountable pain, especially since she had allowed herself to start believing after last night in bed that Dominic might really care for her—that perhaps his attraction was more than just fascination.

Sophie sensed her heart twist with grief. Unwittingly she'd started to let down a few barriers and open her heart to Dominic, and now there was nothing she could do but admit to herself that she loved him. But the devastating words that Diana had expressed would wound anyone who cared deeply about someone else, and Sophie *was* hurt, without a doubt.

'You believe that Dominic can't possibly care about someone like me?' she asked quietly, her heart trying to fend off the sting.

'I don't want to hurt you, Sophie. That's the whole point. But you don't move in the same world as he does. You don't see what I see. Isn't it better you find out the truth about Dominic's character now, rather than later when your heart is in tatters?'

Was that why Dominic had suggested the six-month trial period? Sophie thought frantically now. Was it because he knew that he couldn't possibly stay faithful to someone like her for long? He might desire her above any other woman right now, because he'd become infatuated with her, but he was an intelligent, experienced man—he surely knew that his obsession for Sophie would not last.

'So what are you telling me? That he's a man who can't be trusted where women are concerned?'

'What do *you* think? I'm not trying to cast aspersions on his character, but with Dominic's good looks and immense personal fortune what reason would he have to settle down with any one woman? He's still young—he has plenty of time yet to play the field.'

'And yet despite all of that he *does* want a relationship with me! I never thought I'd find someone I really cared about, Diana...you know that. But I do have *feelings* for Dominic. Can't you just wish me well, like I did you and Freddie, and be happy for me?'

Diana said nothing for several moments. Then finally, throwing Sophie a disparaging glance, the blonde let her true thoughts be known.

'Who do you think you are, believing you can just walk right in and have someone like Dominic at the drop of a hat? To go from near poverty to unimaginable luxury in the blink of an eyelid just like that! Freddie and I have had to work hard for everything we've got...it hasn't just been handed to us on a plate!'

Hardly able to believe what she was hearing, Sophie tried desperately to gather her thoughts. It was just plain laughable if Diana truly believed that good fortune had been handed to Sophie on a plate. She'd worked hard too, and her parents had worked harder still to help her pay her way through college and university, making all kinds of sacrifices along the way. Diana, in contrast, came from a professional background—her parents were doctors. One practised in Harley Street and the other in a private clinic in Chelsea. If she'd had to struggle for the things she wanted at all, it was perhaps because

Freddie spent most of their money trying to fund a life-style that was obviously beyond their means. Finances had been the cause of most of the rows and breakups the two had had.

It was painfully clear to Sophie that her friend was extremely jealous of the idea of Sophie moving 'out of her class' and being with someone like Dominic. The realisation that her friend scorned her humble beginnings was like a brutal slap in the face.

'I'm sorry you've reacted the way you have, Diana. Now that I know what your true feelings are about me there's no sense in you staying, is there? Perhaps you'd better just leave.'

'And when I see Dominic I'll tell him exactly what I think of this whole pathetic fiasco, too!'

As Diana swept from the room out into the hallway, and practically slammed the front door off its hinges, Sophie very much doubted she would tell Dominic any such thing. Diana had always made it known that she was paid a very good salary for being PA to the Dutch billionaire. She doubted if her former friend would jeopardise that salary by telling Dominic exactly what she thought—no matter how vehemently she thought it.

'So, you're moving your pretty little Sophie in with you, are you? I suppose I should take my hat off to her. She's managed what no other girl has managed since I've known you! Are you certain this is what you want, Dominic?'

Smiling her typically wise smile, Emily Cathcart considered her very handsome lunch date with undisguised affection. It wouldn't have been an exaggeration to say that she'd been shocked to her very shoes to hear from Dominic's own lips that he intended to move his new lover in with him, and soon. And it had come as even more of a surprise to learn that the lucky girl was Sophie Dalton—the pretty primary school teacher that Emily had gladly helped kit out with a posh frock for Dominic's presentation at the Guildhall.

She wondered now if Dominic had any idea how this shocking news would send tremors of disbelief vibrating through the circles they both moved in? Dominic Van Straten had been quite the catch for several years now. There wasn't a single ambitious mother in Emily's entire acquaintance, with daughters of marriageable age, who hadn't hoped and dreamed that one day he would make them the most delighted of mothers-in-law.

Lord, but they were going to be greviously disappointed when they found out he'd moved his new lover in with him!

'I am not in the habit of making snap decisions, as you well know, Emily. Yes. I *am* quite certain that this is what I want. And, contrary to what people might believe, I have actually had a hell of a time trying to persuade Sophie that it is a good idea!' Dominic's mouth twisted wryly.

'You mean she resisted the idea of living with you?'

'It seems so.'

'I have to ask, seeing as it seems pertinent—are you in love with the girl, Dominic?'

Seeing no other reason that made sense for him to move the beguiling primary school teacher in with him, Emily satisfied herself that her supposition must be true—even though it was still hard to believe.

In love? Dominic didn't know about that. What did 'in love' mean, exactly? His father had schooled him so thoroughly in the art of containing emotion and not giving any credence to it that it was hard to know. He *did* know that Sophie was the most exciting and sensual creature who had come his way in a very long time: she was bright and without artifice, she hadn't set her cap at him for his fortune, and in bed they aroused each other to fever-pitch.

Dominic had no doubt he was *infatuated* with her. He'd met her at a time in his life when he no longer wanted to be alone—a time when he felt the need to share his life with someone, at long last. And Sophie perfectly fitted the bill. Yes...he had plenty of very persuasive reasons for making his little spitfire his mistress. Even just the thought of her could engender a tug of longing inside his chest. *But 'in love'?*

'You seem to be taking an inordinately long time answering the question, Dominic.'

Frowning, Emily reached for her wine and took a sip, her pale blue eyes considering her companion over the rim of her glass with concern.

'Of course I *care* for her, Emily. She is delightful, if you want to know the truth. You met her, so you must know that. She doesn't bore me, and she will no doubt keep me on my toes for a very long time. I think we will do very well together.'

'And how do you think a girl with no knowledge or experience of the kind of world you move in will cope with all the demands that that world throws at her?'

'I will teach her to cope. I told you she is very bright. I'm sure it will not be a problem.'

'And what about her own career?' Emily persisted, sadly seeing nothing but potholes ahead for the pair of them, because she knew the demanding nature of the man seated in front of her. 'She told me she loves her job. Do you think she'd be willing to give it up to put your needs first, Dominic?'

Dominic's hand tightened briefly round the stem of his wine glass, the question discomfiting him perhaps more than it should. 'She will have to,' he said, his green eyes slowly turning to resolute steel.

As she waited in the drawing room for Dominic to join her after his long-distance phone call, Sophie was still trying to shake off the horrible things that Diana had said to her and, worse, hating the fact that her doubts about being with Dominic had escalated. She was living in la-la land if she imagined this impending arrangement of theirs could possibly work.

Could she, in all honesty, envisage travelling to the primary school where she taught from this palatial house in Mayfair and trying to keep up the semblance of a normal life? And what would her colleagues think when they found out? She didn't have to be a brain surgeon to know that not everyone would be glad for her. If someone she'd considered a very good friend had not been able to wish her well, then what hope for people who knew her less well?

Twisting her hands together, Sophie walked around the room, her gaze alighting with interest and awe on some of the beautiful *objets d'art* on display in the walnut cabinets. There were pieces from all around the globe, which told her that Dominic must have been practically everywhere. What would he say if she told him that she'd only ever been abroad once? And that had been on a camping trip to France!

Her gaze lifted to study some of the stunning art that covered the walls. Feeling increasingly on edge, she let her glance settle on a lone birthday card in the middle of the mantelpiece. She moved towards it, her expression curious. Glancing behind her, to check that Dominic hadn't returned to the room, Sophie picked up the card, opened it, and read the words inside.

To Dominic on your thirty-sixth birthday. Best wishes from your parents.

He'd said nothing to Sophie about it being his birthday. He'd just invited her round for dinner, which his housekeeper was currently preparing. But, even more than feeling surprised because it was his birthday and he hadn't mentioned it, Sophie was stunned that he should receive such a curt, lukewarm greeting on his special day from his own mother and father. *Were they usually this formal with their own son? This cold?* Her heart constricting, she shivered and returned the card to its lonely place on the mantel.

Just as she did so, Dominic returned to the room. Sophie's gaze gravitated to him immediately. How could it not? Tonight he appeared to be even more handsome than ever, dressed casually in informal jeans and sweater, his shoulders filling out the deep blue cashmere with maximum heart-stopping impact.

'I didn't know it was your birthday,' Her smile was tentative as his expression seemed briefly to darken.

'I don't really celebrate birthdays, so it is not so big a deal.'

'Why not?' Immediately concerned, Sophie narrowed her blue eyes.

Shrugging, Dominic just stared back at her for a long moment, trying to garner his feelings on the matter and experiencing a very odd sense of embarrassment about being confronted with it.

'Why not? Because I choose not to. That's why not.'

He knew he sounded testy, and he disliked himself for it.

'That's no reason. I should think getting another year older and finding yourself in good health and in good circumstances is very much worth celebrating. I *always* celebrate my birthdays. It's the one day in the year that I make a point of having the day off work, if it falls on a weekday. And my mum always makes me a cake.'

'Lucky you.'

His sarcasm caused a spasm of pain to jolt inside Sophie's chest. Swallowing hard, she tried to rise above it. 'If you'd told me it was your birthday *I* would have made you a cake myself.'

'By all means make me a cake, if it makes you happy.'

He strode across the room to the drinks cabinet and poured a generous measure of Scotch into a tumbler. Watching him, Sophie wished she didn't feel like crying, but suddenly everything seemed so futile. She'd endured enough unpleasantness for one day and really didn't want to endure any more—least of all Dominic's hostility.

'Does it not appeal to you, my making you a cake?' she asked softly, trying to will him back into a more amenable mood.

Rounding on her, his green eyes cool as a glacier, Dominic put the tumbler of whisky to his lips and drank some before speaking. 'Why should it, when I can order myself a cake from the best bakery in the country if I wish? Or even from France?'

'*That's* not the same thing at all!'

Stung, Sophie stared at him as if she couldn't believe what she was hearing. 'Are you so far above everyone else that you can't see that something made with love is worth far more than something you can easily purchase with money?'

'Who said anything about love?'

His expression didn't warm one iota. If anything it became even colder. Shocked by his apparent disdain for her opinion, and his blatant disregard for her feelings, Sophie felt her feet were rooted to the floor.

'I didn't mean—that is to say I—' Struggling as the misery inside her escalated with the realisation that Dominic scorned the mere idea that she could love him, Sophie blinked hard to keep back her tears.

Leaving aside his drink, he stalked over to her and clasped her gently on either side of her arms. 'Make me a cake by all means—I'm sure it would be wonderful.'

But even as he spoke Dominic sensed that his placatory remarks might have come too late. Seeing tears shimmering in her lovely eyes, he wished he hadn't let his irritable mood taint their time together.

Sophie's mention of love had been a mere slip of the tongue, he was sure—her naïve way of trying to make him feel better. Added to that, he'd just heard from Geneva that there were problems already arising concerning the deal he'd struck, and it didn't exactly make him feel like dancing for joy. Now he was probably going to have to make a return trip to Switzerland to sort things out.

'It doesn't matter.' Sophie sighed. 'I'm hardly going to inflict my humble offering on you when you can easily buy some fabulous creation from Paris or somewhere! Let me go, Dominic. I want to go home.'

Immediately Dominic dropped his hands to his sides. 'I invited you to dinner,' he said through terse lips, irritated that she would not be so easily won round after his attempt at making the peace. 'And we have to talk about your moving in.'

'Well, I've changed my mind about staying. Clearly you'd prefer to dine alone on your birthday. Judging by the mood you're in, I'd say it was probably for the best anyway.'

'Don't leave. I might have to return to Geneva tomorrow. I don't know how long I'll be gone, and we might have to delay your moving in until I get back.' His brow creasing in frustration, Dominic found it hard to find a smile to coax Sophie into staying. Then an idea came to him—one that made increasing sense as it grew inside him.

'Come *with* me. Meetings will take up most of the day, but I always have a car at my disposal so you can do some sightseeing. Then in the evenings we can be together.'

Seeing the leap of hope in his eyes, Sophie nonetheless knew it was impossible. Plus, she didn't exactly feel eager to forgive him after the rebuff she'd received over her suggestion of making him a cake.

'I can't. Tomorrow the children are putting on a special Easter play for the parents. We've been rehearsing. Then the next day they're performing it for the rest of the school. It's a busy time for me.'

Biting her lip, she turned away, walking over to the couch where she had left her handbag.

'Have you forgotten about our arrangement? Surely I deserve more consideration than that? Or will your job always take precedence over the needs of our relationship?'

Hurt that he could believe she would be so intransigent, Sophie frowned. 'As part of a couple, of course I would always strive to compromise when things like this come up. Unfortunately the Easter celebrations are pretty much set in stone, Dominic. Performing in the play means a lot to the children. They've been rehearsing for weeks, and as their teacher I'm the only one who knows what's to be done. I couldn't possibly take time off during such a crucial time.'

She *hated* the fact that he was going away again when he had only just returned, but she was wary about expressing her true feelings when Dominic seemed to be setting the standard for the way their relationship would progress. He wasn't interested in her love. He desired her, and he wanted her to be with him because he was used to getting whatever he wanted *when* he wanted it, but so far he had not expressed any spirit of compromise whatsoever. The more she realised it, the more Sophie sensed their union could bring nothing but disaster for them both.

Her chest felt as if it had a huge rock inside it as Dominic's frosty gaze swept over her.

'So you won't come with me to Geneva?'

'I told you—I can't!'

'Then so be it. But when I return you and I are going to have to have a very serious talk.'

Did he mean that he was going to call off their plans? That he never wanted to see her again? Sophie knew she couldn't wait for however long Dominic was away in Geneva to hear the truth. The waiting and the nervous expectation of hearing the worst would likely *kill* her.

'Why don't we have that talk right now, rather than wait until you get back from Geneva?' Clutching her leather handbag stiffly between her fingers, Sophie stood her ground, feeling as if a chill factor of below zero had just swept in from the Arctic.

Used to calling the shots, Dominic would not be

moved. Even though he'd witnessed the treacherous wobble of her vulnerable bottom lip as she stood facing him, clearly expecting the worst. It hit him then that she must imagine he was going to suggest they part. The fact that Dominic intended no such thing, but merely wanted to lay down some important ground rules for their future relationship, caused relief and adrenaline suddenly to flood through his system. But it surely wouldn't hurt to play her along a little bit? It might after all make her think twice about putting the demands of her job over their relationship.

'No. We will wait until I return. Now, are you going to stay for dinner or not?'

Walking to the door, her head held determinedly high even though her heart was breaking, Sophie turned briefly to regard Dominic as he stood by the fireplace, beside that ominous lone birthday card that resided on the mantel.

'I'm not. Have a safe trip, won't you?'

CHAPTER ELEVEN

IT ATE at Sophie's soul that Dominic would be spending his birthday eating dinner alone. There he was, a man with more advantages and material assets than most people could dream of, and yet tonight he was all on his own in that big glamorous house in Mayfair, with just one abstemious birthday card from his parents on the mantel.

Did his friends not think Dominic's birthday was worth celebrating? Or perhaps he didn't *tell* them when his birthday was?

'It's not so big a deal,' he had explained, almost disdainfully. *But what if he hadn't meant that at all?* Sophie considered thoughtfully. What if secretly he would *enjoy* being made a fuss of on his birthday? If his parents were so reserved with their good wishes, perhaps he'd grown up taking their lead, and believing that birthdays weren't a big deal? But that didn't stop him from minding that they weren't celebrated.

Sophie's thoughts feverishly ran on. And if people around him perceived him as the man who had everything, how would they believe that he *needed* anything? Like simple good wishes and fun on his birthday? It was Sophie's opinion that when she'd left him Dominic had not looked like a man who had everything at all. She'd been left with the impression of something quite different.

The ridiculous feeling that she'd somehow abandoned him on his birthday wouldn't leave her alone for the rest of the evening. Finally, unable to bear her incessant fretting, Sophie ran herself a hot bath to distract herself. But as she lay back in the fragrant lapping water, trying hard to will the tensions of the day away, an even more worrying thought wormed its way into her thinking.

What if Dominic hadn't stayed alone when she'd left? What if he'd rung some *glamorous* female friend of his who was more than willing to come over and keep him company? Diana had more or less intimated that he was inundated by phone calls from women throughout any one week. What did that signify? That he could take his pick of women whenever he wanted? Surely they couldn't all just be 'friends'? Sophie groaned out loud in dismay. Unable to enjoy even the apparently uncomplicated simple pleasure of a long hot soak, she got out of the bath and with a heavy heart dried herself, then dressed in her night things and deliberately went to bed.

Returning the telephone receiver to its rest, Dominic rubbed ruefully at his throbbing ear. Having just spent the entire morning on a call to Geneva, trying to circumvent the need to fly out there at least for the next few days, he had achieved his object with not a small amount of difficulty.

The decision to postpone his trip had been reached last night, after barely doing justice to the beautiful dinner Maria had cooked for him. *A dinner he'd hoped to share with Sophie.* After he'd eaten Dominic had spent the rest of the evening in morose contemplation, finally picking up the birthday card he'd received from his parents, tearing it up and throwing the pieces in the bin.

He'd wanted to go round to Sophie's place there and then, to tell her that he'd rather spend the evening of his birthday with her than anybody else and apologise for

being such a boor. But stubborn pride had stopped him.
He wasn't used to admitting he might have been at fault,
and he certainly wasn't used to apologising. And his
antipathy to publicly owning to either of those two traits
was so strong that he'd made himself spend the entire
evening wallowing in misery rather than doing what his
heart really desired.

However, *today* was a different matter. Having postponed the need to go to Geneva, Dominic vowed to do
something about this intended agreement of theirs—and
do it *now*. He picked up the telephone receiver once
more and dialled out.

On playground duty, Sophie did up another button on
her coat and crossed her arms in front of her chest to
keep warm. The day—though bright—was particularly
cold, and she envied the children tearing around—having fun, keeping warm, and paying no mind to the in-
clement temperature as only children could.

'Please, Miss... That man over there is waving to
you.'

'Ashley!' Smiling down at the pretty five-year-old
with her blonde curls, Sophie strained to hear the soft,
sweet voice. 'What did you say?'

Crouching down to give her full attention to the child,
she felt her heart start to beat wildly when she saw the
little girl point to Dominic, standing outside the gates of
the playground gazing in at her. The collar of his mack-
intosh was turned up, and his expression was hard to
detect at the distance that separated them.

She couldn't believe he'd turned up at the school.
Wasn't he supposed to be flying out to Geneva today?
Fearful of what had brought him, and wondering what
he was going to say, Sophie thanked the child and made

her way towards him, self-consciously trying to pat down her wind-blown hair as she approached.

'Dominic! What are you doing here? I thought you were going to Geneva?'

'I postponed my trip. I rang the school office to speak to you, and they told me you were on playground duty. I wanted to meet you after school. I thought we could go and have coffee somewhere and talk?'

Even though they'd parted on uneasy terms, and she was still feeling sore, Sophie couldn't think of a single excuse to deny him just then. In truth, she was too happy that he *hadn't* left on his trip.

'Okay,' she agreed. 'School finishes in about an hour. I'll see you then.'

'Good.'

With an unexpected smile he briefly inclined his head, glancing over her shoulder at the children playing. 'Looks like you've got your hands full,' he commented wryly.

Something about that smile—the wary, almost cautious nature of it—as if he fully expected his conversational stance to be rebuffed—tore at Sophie's heart and caused her own enforced wariness to relent. Her lips parted in one of her brightest, sunniest grins.

'You don't know the half of it! But at least they're keeping warm tearing around, while I'm standing out here doing a good impression of an icicle!'

'I'll have to think of something to warm you up when I see you, in that case.' Dominic's emerald eyes briefly darkened, with palpable need and a flare of heat inside Sophie suddenly chased away the cold and made her tremble with longing.

'I'd better go. I daren't take my eyes off of this lot for a second!' She started to withdraw.

'After school then... Bye.'

He turned and walked away. Sophie watched him as he quickened his pace to cross the road: a tall, impressive figure with a bright crown of golden hair that would catch the eye of even the most short-sighted woman in the world and make her heart beat faster at the mere sight of him.

Louis opened the door of the Rolls and was ready at the kerbside waiting to help Sophie as she stepped out, closely followed by Dominic. Curious, she glanced around the busy London thoroughfare with its impressive array of up-market shops—mostly selling the kind of expensive items that she couldn't dream of buying on a teacher's pay—and wondered where Dominic was going to take her for coffee.

When he lightly touched the small of her back to direct her towards a nearby jeweller's, Sophie's shock was palpable. Especially when she read the inscription 'Jewellers to Her Majesty the Queen'.

Deliberately slowing on the pavement beside him, Sophie knew her blue eyes were clearly troubled as she commanded his attention. 'Where are you taking me, Dominic? I thought you said we were going somewhere for coffee?'

'I want to buy you some jewellery, Sophie—something to seal our agreement. Is that all right with you? I have made an appointment and we are expected.'

Sophie had truly believed that he was going to call the whole thing off, and instead he was professing to buy her yet another expensive gift—to 'seal' their agreement. She seriously needed a few moments to acclimatise herself to the idea. Last night Dominic had been morose and withdrawn, and what else should she have thought other than that he wanted to rescind his proposition? Indeed, Sophie had been mentally gearing herself up to hear him say the words that would no doubt herald the worst misery she had ever experienced.

But now, as she glanced at his usually guarded expression, she saw an intention blazing in his arresting gaze that couldn't help but make her hopes soar. 'After last night… I thought you might be having reservations about me coming to live with you,' she confessed, her eyes sliding away from his.

Because he had experienced the same doubt about Sophie's feelings towards him, Dominic experienced a strong upsurge of fierce satisfaction that she was still willing to go through with their agreement. *Especially* when he had behaved like such a jerk towards her last night. If she *had* changed her mind about their living together he would not have known what to do, he realised. For once in his life he would have been at a complete loss.

When he'd seen her in the playground of the school this afternoon, with the children running around her and her lovely face never wavering far from a smile, something hard inside him had melted. Like a large chunk of ice succumbing to spring sunshine. For a long moment the feeling had left him breathless. That unfamiliar *warmth* inside of him when he gazed at Sophie had illustrated with impact that her rejection would have been untenable. It would have seriously pained Dominic to let her go.

He had *never* felt such an attachment to anyone before—including his parents. It made him even more determined to have her by his side and introduce her to the privileged world he inhabited. No matter how cynical or shocked by his choice of lover his friends or family might be when they heard the news.

'We had an agreement, yes? I have no intention of reneging on it. It is what I *want*.'

It was not the answer that Sophie's heart ached for. Admirable though it undoubtedly was that Dominic was a man of integrity and honour, they were *not* the qualities she needed him to demonstrate right then. When he urged her onwards to their destination Sophie held back, hurt and doubt clouding her beautiful blue eyes as she continued to study him.

'Wait a minute, Dominic. We shouldn't just rush into this. More important than you buying me another gift is the fact that we need to talk about *us*.'

Surprise flitted across his handsome face. 'How much talking do we need to do, Sophie? We both know what we feel towards each other, don't we? I want you to move in with me, and the sooner we organise that the better.'

'That's what I mean, Dominic! You're making a lot of assumptions without even consulting me! It's just not practical for me to live in Mayfair—don't you realise that? Where I live right now, my school is only a bus ride away. It would take me twice as long to get there every day from your house!'

'Why are you worrying about bus rides? You can easily drive to school from where I live.'

It had seriously started to alarm Dominic that Sophie would even *think* of remaining in her own small house when they had already made what he considered to be a firm agreement that she would move in with him. She simply seemed set on creating difficulties where as far as he could see there *weren't* any.

'I can't drive anywhere Dominic...I don't have a car!

And, besides that, the West End traffic is too horrendous to make that feasible even if I *did* have one.'

'You're deliberately making a problem where there isn't one!' he concluded impatiently, drawing her away to the relative shelter of a shopfront awning, out of the jostling of hurrying passers-by. 'I'll happily buy you a car of your choice. And if you choose not to drive yourself to work I'll get Louis to drive you.'

Dominic didn't reveal to Sophie that he fully intended for her eventually to give up working as a teacher...quite *soon* after she moved in with him in, fact. So the thorny issue about how she would get there every day would no longer be a problem. He had months of business travel ahead, and he wanted Sophie with him. He had no intention of enjoying a relationship with her only to leave her behind when he went to work. Not when he wanted to experience more of this bewitching warmth he was feeling around her.

Sophie just about stopped herself from laughing out loud. The very idea that she would be dropped off each day at the school where she worked by Louis, driving the Rolls, was so ludicrous that it was like some unbelievable scenario in a comedy programme! But, staring dumbfounded into Dominic's completely serious face, she realised that the anomaly had not even struck him. He *was* just as she'd suspected that first day they had met, when she'd been splashed by that muddy puddle and Louis had pulled over. Protected by vast wealth and a lifestyle so far removed from the everyday concerns of most folk, he had no *idea* of the problems such a showy display of wealth might bring.

She would have happily been able to overlook the odd eccentricity on his part if he had loved her. But no amount of wishing and hoping would persuade Sophie now that there was even a possibility of such an event. Dominic wanted what he wanted, and right now, for some inexplicable reason, he wanted Sophie.

She had to ask herself would she be happy just being another acquisition for him, like some of those beautiful objets d'art in his walnut cabinets? She knew the answer straight away. Women like Diana might be open to entertaining such a situation, in return for experiencing wealth beyond their wildest dreams, but Sophie *wasn't*.

'Dominic, I really don't want to think about buying jewellery right now. Can you ask Louis to just drop me home…please? If that's not possible, I'll catch the tube.'

Sensing her determined withdrawal, Dominic felt shock and fury lace his gut in an angry cocktail. 'I cannot believe you are doing this! We had an agreement!'

A little vein in his forehead throbbed, and a wave of sadness rolled over Sophie at the realisation that he was probably just disappointed by not having his wishes fulfilled. If he had told her he needed her—or cared for her, even—she might have relented to this 'six-month' arrangement he'd been proposing. She might even have allowed herself to believe that Dominic *might* grow to love her eventually, and that they could make their union a happy and long-lasting one. But all she saw on his beguiling, handsome face right then was the petulant displeasure of a man who was not accustomed to being thwarted in any way.

'Some agreements *must* be open to renegotiation, Dominic. And this is one of them. You and I are too different to have a hope of making a relationship work. I think you really know that in your heart. You seem to see a relationship as something purely pragmatic, to fulfil a need, and I don't. As much as I've been hurt in the past, I don't want to give up on the idea of falling in love and spending the rest of my days with that person…rich or *poor*. I'm sure you'll think that's very naïve of me, and you're entitled to your opinion, but that's what *I* want. From what Diana has intimated you won't be without female company for long. Don't worry about giving me a lift. I'd rather catch the tube.'

And before Dominic could gather his wits and try and reason with her Sophie had joined the throng of passers-by travelling in the opposite direction. She was hurrying away from him, her expression determined, as if she couldn't escape quickly enough.

What had Sophie meant when she'd suggested that he wouldn't be without female company for long?

Pacing the large, some would say intimidating room that was his personal office, Dominic glanced out at the teeming rain that fell past his window and strove hard to will his misery away.

He'd been dissecting every part of their last conversation. From her accusation that he thought of a relationship between them as 'purely pragmatic,' to fulfil a need, to her confession that, in spite of being hurt in the past, she'd never given up hope of falling in love and spending the rest of her life with someone. *Rich or poor.*

He'd had sleepless nights because of that last part. Dominic wanted Sophie to fall in love with nobody but *him.* That desire had also come as a revelation. To realise that what he'd actually been craving all along was Sophie's love. He'd never wanted that from any woman before. He hadn't even believed in it. 'Emotions are notoriously unreliable,' his father had always taught him, and so Dominic had steered clear of emotional involvement ever since. Now he saw what *bad* advice he'd been given. He was tired of being alone. He *wanted* emotional involvement. He wanted it with Sophie.

Sighing, he remembered that Sophie had actually said that *Diana* had intimated that he wouldn't be without female company for long. If that was the case, then his assistant must have been discussing him with Sophie—and not in a good way, either.

Before he gave himself time to consider the thought further, he pulled open the adjoining door that separated his own office from his personal assistant's and marched straight over to her desk. In the middle of a phone call, Diana mimed, *Just a minute*, as Dominic leant over her, and was completely taken aback when he grabbed the receiver from her hand and slammed it down on its rest.

'What have you been saying to Sophie?' he demanded, his eyes glittering hard. At the sight of the swift colour that invaded the blonde's otherwise pale cheeks Dominic instinctively knew she had not been painting him in the best of lights to her friend.

'I don't know what you mean, Dominic.'

Her hazel eyes slightly panicked, Diana strove hard to retain her usually famous composure. Dominic blew hot and cold, she knew that. He could lose his temper with her one minute, then buy her a gift or treat her to lunch the next, in gratitude for all her hard work.

'Did you suggest to her that I might be seeing other women?' He came straight to the point, his chest constricted with fury that his own PA might have soured things for him with the woman he wanted to be with.

Dominic knew he'd played his part in driving Sophie away. He was quite aware that he'd tried to steamroller her into moving in with him, scarcely taking her wants and needs into consideration at all. But two days had gone by since she'd left him standing outside the jeweller's in Grafton Street, and he'd had plenty of time for reflection about what had happened, since. *He hadn't liked what he'd discovered about himself, that much was certain. But he didn't like being lied about either.*

It was true he had many female friends, but he certainly wasn't having sexual relations with any of them. Other than the odd one-night stand, to meet the most basic of functions, he'd steered clear of personal involvement until he'd met Sophie!

'I said that sometimes other women rang you at work,' Diana admitted, reddening even more. 'But when I said that I wasn't trying to suggest that you were having relationships with those women, Dominic.'

'And if you were in Sophie's shoes, and a friend said that to you, what would *you* think she meant?'

Before she could answer his question, Dominic swung away from the desk and paced to the other side of the room and back. 'I have a feeling that you have been saying other things to Sophie, Diana...perhaps not very complimentary things about me? Is that right?'

Feeling herself pushed into a corner, Diana sighed in exasperation. 'What you must understand about Sophie, Dominic, is that although she's a teacher, she's actually quite naïve in many respects. Sadly, she has some ridiculous idea that you want her to move in with you! Naturally I had to help her come to her senses.'

'*Naturally.*'

Dominic didn't know how he held onto his temper as he stared at the ice-cool blonde whose secretarial and organisational abilities had, up until now, always impressed him. 'If Sophie told you that that was what I wanted, why didn't you believe her? Is your friend accustomed to telling you lies?'

Seeing Diana flinch at that, Dominic was even more

furious with the woman for letting Sophie down than himself. Knowing the kind of warm, generous person Sophie was, he concluded that she deserved far *better* friends than Diana.

'Anyway, she told me she didn't want to get involved with another man for a long time! Her previous boyfriend went to bed with his best friend's girlfriend, and Sophie was devastated. She's totally cynical about relationships. I even had to practically blackmail her into coming to my wedding, she disapproves of them so much! And then she turned up covered in mud, looking like she'd been on an assault course with the army!'

Out of pure frustration and annoyance with Sophie, for putting her in such an awkward position with her boss, Diana was resorting to plain vindictiveness to protect herself. It made Dominic see his personal assistant in an entirely different light from the one he'd seen her in before, and he didn't *like* what he saw. No matter how busy or in demand he was, he'd always prided himself in choosing good staff. He liked to think that he had reasonably good intuition, as well as first-class interviewing skills when it came to the selection process. Now he realised that he might have made a mistake where Diana was concerned.

In Dominic's opinion, although he didn't ever particularly strive to be liked by anyone, he viewed loyalty to one's friends as paramount—unless it was proved in some way that that loyalty was misplaced. Diana had more than demonstrated that she felt no loyalty towards Sophie whatsoever. If she had badmouthed Dominic in any way to her, then clearly she did *not* have Sophie's interests at heart. Yes, Dominic had female friends that he occasionally liked to wine and dine, but true to his word he had mostly avoided more intimate associations because all they did was leave him feeling soulless. *Until Sophie…*

'I think you owe your friend Sophie an apology.' His voice was level, but his blazing green eyes nonetheless spoke volumes as he settled them on Diana. 'Knowing the kind of person she is, no doubt she will accept it. But I truly hope, for her sake, that she has nothing whatsoever to do with you again after that. In light of the current situation, we need to have a very serious talk Mrs Carmichael. Ten o'clock tomorrow morning in my office. Don't be late.'

Before Diana could even blink in astonishment, Dominic had stalked back into his office and slammed the door.

CHAPTER TWELVE

'SOPHIE…might I have a word?'

Victor Edwards's calm tones cut through the fog that had descended on her mind, and Sophie glanced up from the text on childcare she'd been only half reading. Still in a daze, she pushed to her feet.

'Of course.'

Following him out of the staffroom and along the echoing tiled corridor to the headmaster's office, Sophie was glad that Victor was mainly silent, because she really didn't feel like talking much. In his office he offered her a chair and a cup of coffee, and while he attended to the pouring of the coffee she tried hard to will her expression into one of composure. Unfortunately she knew that right now her emotions were precariously poised on a cliff-edge, and she hoped that whatever he had to say wasn't going to open the floodgates and tip her over.

It had been a week since she'd left Dominic standing outside the jeweller's and walked away. *A whole week and since then…nothing. No letter or phone call. Not even to acknowledge that what they had had between them was over. And each day that passed seemed like a lifetime…*

'There you are. White, one sugar—just as you like it.'

Beaming at her like some kind of fond uncle, Victor carefully placed the cup and saucer on the desk between them. Retrieving his own drink, he sat in the somewhat tired-looking leather chair that had been an integral part of his office for years, and linked his hands together in front of him.

'How long have you been with us, Sophie? I think it's three years now, isn't it?'

Where was this leading? Looking across at him, her attention suddenly switching to full alertness, Sophie blinked. 'I can hardly believe it myself but, yes…it is three years.'

'And you have enjoyed your time with us?'

Shifting uncomfortably in her seat, Sophie's spine prickled in anxiety at what might be coming next.

'I've enjoyed it very much. Is there something wrong, Headmaster? Is it something to do with my work?'

She really hoped not. No matter how she was feeling—good or bad—Sophie always strove to give of her best once she was in the classroom with the children. They might come from all kinds of family backgrounds, each with their own attendant problems, but the kids wouldn't ever receive negative vibes from her.

'There's nothing wrong, Sophie, and especially not concerning your work. No, my dear, I am sorry if I've alarmed you unwittingly. It's just that I know how dedicated you are, and how eager you are to progress, and a post has come up in another school that I think you might well be interested in. As much as I would hate to lose you, I thought it was only right to bring it to your attention.'

Victor paused for a moment to glean Sophie's reaction. Momentarily mesmerised by the startling cornflower-blue of her pretty eyes, he quickly glanced away to rifle through some papers on the desk in front of him. Then, regaining his composure, he gave Sophie a brief smile. 'Now, the position won't actually be available for another six months, but in the meantime they are interviewing prospective candidates, and if you are interested I would be very happy to arrange an interview on your behalf.'

Her interest definitely captured, Sophie leaned forward in her seat, her gloom put determinedly aside as she listened to Victor outline the very appealing benefits of this new post in another school...

Immersed in stripping wallpaper off the walls in the living room, in a bid to spring-clean her life, Sophie cursed beneath her breath when someone rang on the doorbell. She hated being interrupted when she had the bit between her teeth, but she wiped her wet hands down the front of her faded jeans and baggy overshirt and went to see who'd had the audacity to disturb her.

'Diana!'

All kinds of emotions clamoured inside Sophie at the sight of her friend, but the one most prevalent was sadness. They'd been friends for about four years now, since Sophie had temped as a secretary in the summer holidays leading up to her final exams. They were very different people, but somehow they had hit it off. Diana had introduced Sophie to lots of new and exciting experiences, and the two women had had fun together. Now, Sophie was shocked to find her at her door, a not-so-confident smile on her attractive face, and holding out a bouquet of spring flowers.

Sophie kept her hands deliberately down by her sides. 'What can I do for you?'

'I've been a bitch. I know it. I've come round to apologise and to tell you that I would like to be your friend again. Any chance?' Grimacing, Diana held out the flowers again.

Sophie accepted them...albeit reluctantly. It didn't

mean, however, that she was going to run full-tilt back into a full-on friendship with Diana again. Diana had said some dreadful things, that had really hurt, and Sophie realised that though she was willing to forgive, it wouldn't be so easy to forget. Pushing her fringe out of her eyes, she briefly sniffed the perfume emanating from the flowers and tried to get a handle on her emotions. Since she'd broken up with Dominic she'd turned into a real water fountain—crying at the drop of a hat at the slightest thing. Even though she'd told herself it was pathetic, she couldn't seem to help herself.

'I need some time to think about that, Diana,' she said quietly.

The blonde frowned. 'Can't I come in for just a minute? I can't talk to you properly out here on the doorstep.'

'I'm decorating, and everywhere is in a mess.'

'I don't care. It's you I've come to see, not your house!'

'Just for a minute, then. I really need to get on.'

Her chest feeling hollow, Sophie turned and walked back down the corridor, then turned off into the kitchen. She put the flowers in the sink and ran some water into the basin around the stems. Hearing Diana come in behind her, she turned slowly and folded her arms across her chest. Diana appeared as immaculate as usual—her make-up perfect, looking slim and elegant in an understated black trouser suit with a cream camisole. In comparison, dressed in her old jeans and shirt, with vestiges of dust in her hair, Sophie knew she must look a fright.

'What did you want to talk about?'

'Apart from telling you again that I'm truly sorry for the abominable way I behaved? *Dominic.*'

'What about Dominic?' Striving to keep her voice

level, not to let the other woman see how his name alone could unravel her, Sophie stared.

'He loves you.'

'What did you say?'

'I said he loves you! All those things I said to you, I said because I was jealous. You're pretty as a peach, you've got a great figure, and a career you love—and then someone like Dominic comes along and snaps you up! Not *that* many women ring him up at work, Sophie, and the ones who do are only friends. I promise. I've been his PA for three and a bit years now. If he was having a relationship with any of them don't you think I'd know?'

All Sophie had really heard was what Diana had said first. *Why was she taunting her with such lies? Hadn't she done enough damage already? Of course Dominic didn't love her!* As far as Sophie was able to conclude, he was *incapable* of loving anyone. Such a tender and strong emotion was just not part of the man's make-up. Whatever he'd learned as a child, it wasn't how to love…

'I don't want to hear any more, Diana. Please, just go, will you? I need to pop out to the hardware shop before it closes, and I don't have time to stand around and chat!'

Striding to the door, Sophie was totally taken aback when Diana caught her by the arm and pulled her back into the room.

'What do you think you're doing?' Shaking her arm free, she felt her cheeks go pink with indignation.

'You idiot!'

'What did you call me?' Hands on her hips, Sophie stared at the other woman as if she'd gone quite mad.

'You're not listening to me, Sophie! Dominic loves you! Doesn't that mean anything to you?'

A week ago it would have meant the whole world...*if it were true*. But, wherever Diana had got her information from, Sophie knew it was clearly a lie. The man hadn't even phoned her to see if she was all right. Was that an example of someone who *loved* her?

'And how do you come to such a blatantly untrue conclusion?'

'Because I've seen how he's been during the past week since you walked away and left him! He's not the most even-tempered guy at the best of times, but in the past week he's been hell on wheels! Do you know I've just about held onto my job by the skin of my teeth?'

Diana shook her head from side to side, remembering the scalding interview she'd had with Dominic where he'd read her the Riot Act and warned her that if she ever interfered in his personal business again she would be looking for another job. He'd told her the only reason he was keeping her on at all was because of her past exemplary record—but one step out of line and that would be it.

'He was furious with me for telling you about other women ringing him up at the office. Since then not a day has passed without him asking me if I've heard from you. Go and see him, Sophie. Put the both of you out of your misery!'

Could what Diana was saying be true? Sophie hardly dared hope. But *if it were true* she still couldn't understand why Dominic had not contacted her first. Then a stunning thought came to her. *Was stubborn pride getting in his way?*

Nobody liked being rejected, and Sophie had walked out on him when he'd been intent on buying her something nice—a piece of jewellery to cement their decision about living together. Even if her reasons had been sound ones, her actions *must* have caused him hurt. She remembered the lone birthday card from his parents on the mantel, the curt, minimalist greeting which was no loving greeting at all, and her heart just about turned over inside her chest with dismay.

'I—I can't just drop in on him unannounced. He might be busy. He might have visitors. He might—'

'Sophie?' Diana grabbed her by the wrists and smiled. 'Stop looking for excuses. Go and change out of those old clothes, put some lippy on and I'll run you over to his place. I'm meeting Freddie for a picnic in Hyde Park, so it's on my way. Now, go!'

'I need to stop off somewhere first. Do you mind?'

Diana gave her a little shove. 'Not if you hurry up!'

'Miss Dalton. What a pleasant surprise.'

Andrews answered the door, an unreserved smile on his lined face as he surveyed a nervous Sophie, standing on the step carrying a large white box.

'Hello, there. I was wondering if Dominic was at home?'

Now she'd come this far Sophie knew she would feel entirely foolish were he *not* at home. She didn't know whether she would be able to pluck up the courage to make a second attempt at a later date. Already adrenaline was shooting through her veins, making her light-headed as she considered the very real possibility that she might have made a terrible mistake.

What if he didn't love her at all? What if all Diana's convincing summations about the state of his feelings towards Sophie were wrong?

'Yes, miss. Mr Van Straten is in the drawing room,'

Andrews replied, holding the door wide for Sophie to come in.

'Is he alone?' She bit her lip, anxious that if he had company she wouldn't get the opportunity to say what she'd come to say.

'Yes, miss. Quite alone.'

Andrews discreetly left her at the drawing room doors with a smile, and told her to go on inside. Waiting until his footsteps had receded down the hall, Sophie took a deep, bolstering breath and, still carrying the white box, opened the door and walked in.

Dominic was seated in an armchair, a newspaper spread out on his knees and his eyes closed. From discreetly placed speakers drifted the languorous sounds of some gentle piano music. As quietly as she could Sophie managed to close the twin doors behind her. As the catch made a soft 'snick' Dominic's eyes flew open, and he stared at Sophie as though she were some ghostly figment of his imagination.

'Sophie.'

He neither smiled nor rose from his chair.

Feeling suddenly unsure about her own temerity, Sophie started to walk towards him. 'I took a chance that you'd be in,' she told him, her voice a little throaty because of nerves. 'I—I hope you didn't mind?'

'Mind?' He swept aside his newspaper and drove his fingers through his hair—as a person would when they were disturbed unexpectedly and were conscious of feeling momentarily vulnerable. But his unfathomable emerald eyes locked unsettlingly onto Sophie's and made her heart jump. 'No. Of course I don't mind.'

For a disturbing moment Dominic felt as if he couldn't breathe. He'd been dreaming about her, and waking to find her there in the flesh had been a shock...*if a wonderful one.* She looked sexy and pretty, in tight blue jeans, white shirt and a pale blue tweed jacket, her dark hair naturally settling softly around her lovely face. *If she is part of my dream still, then please let me dream it a little longer,* he thought with feeling.

'I've brought you something.'

Smiling, she put the box onto his knees and stood back while he lifted the lid to reveal a large iced cake.

'What's this all about?' His voice unwittingly husky, Dominic frowned.

'It's a birthday cake,' Sophie explained, her cheeks turning rose. 'You didn't have one for your birthday, and I thought you should. I'm only sorry that I didn't make it personally. But then again you might well have been sorry if I had. I'm not exactly the world's greatest cook. If my baking does turn out all right, it's more by luck than judgement, I have to say—'

'Sophie?'

'Yes, Dominic?' She stared as he put the box down beside the chair and rose to his full intimidating height. Her pulse started to race.

'Did you come and see me only to bring a cake?'

'No.' Her feet rooted to the floor, Sophie searched her mind desperately for the right words. 'I came to tell you I was sorry I just left you standing there like that. I know you meant well when you said you wanted to buy me something. It's just that everything happened so quickly, and I got scared when I realised what we were contemplating... Especially when you didn't—when you—'

'I love you, Sophie. In fact I'm quite crazy about you. I should have told you when I took you to the jeweller's, but I was scared too.'

'You were?'

'Love makes you vulnerable. I've never been vulnerable in my life, as far as I know. To love someone and to have them love you back—that is an awful risk, Sophie. One I was admittedly too scared to contemplate.'

'Life is a risk, Dominic,' Sophie replied tenderly. 'And as far as I can tell you've embraced that with both hands, or you wouldn't be as successful as you are. I *do* love you. So now I'm taking a risk too. We're in this together, Dominic.'

Sophie stared at him hard, barely daring to believe that this amazing man had just confessed that he loved her and that it scared him.

Stepping towards her, with a gentle brush of his fingers Dominic touched her cheek. 'I never believed in falling in love until I met you,' he admitted, smiling. 'You made me hot, yes. But love? It has quite taken me by surprise. My family are in for quite a shock, I think.'

'They don't believe that you could fall in love either?'

'My parents are pragmatists, Sophie. They never leave anything to chance. But when they meet you and get to know you I hope that they will grow to love you too.'

'Even if they don't, Dominic, it doesn't matter. I'll be quite content just to have your love.' Her voice falling to all but a whisper, Sophie stood up on tiptoes and kissed Dominic gently on the lips.

The touch of her mouth, damp and soft, made him groan and pull her hard into his chest. In just a few explosive seconds, he was on fire for her, his body primed to seduce her, needing the release of hot loving that only she could provide.

But before he could persuade her that making love would be good for both of them—and hopefully she wouldn't need *that* much persuasion—he had to know why Sophie had come back to him. Especially when he'd been certain that all hope of seeing her again was lost.

'How did you know?' he asked, briefly holding her away from him to study the expression in her eyes. 'How did you know that I must be in love with you?'

'Diana came to see me. She more or less told me that she thought you were missing me and had concluded that you must be in love with me.'

Dominic wasn't surprised that Sophie had entertained her friend's company once again. He'd never known a more generous-hearted woman than her. The warmth that he'd grown to feel around her seemed to expand inside his chest. 'Ah.'

'Yes, and I've got something else to tell you too.'

Needing to touch him more intimately, Sophie slid her hand down his shirt, her palm feeling the tremendous heat he exuded with a little thrill inside her. 'I've applied for a new teaching job.'

'Oh?' Knowing that this might be a bone of contention between them, even though they'd agreed they were in love, Dominic studied her animated face with silent reservation. He had several weeks' business travel ahead of him, and he was not looking forward to leaving Sophie behind for even a single day—let alone weeks at a time.

'It's at a progressive new school in Westminster, and if I get the post I'll start in six months' time.'

'Six months?' Dominic grabbed her hand where it was sliding up and down his chest, provoking him into a near spin, and deliberately stilled it. 'What does that mean, Sophie? Does it mean you can take some time off to go on honeymoon?'

'Honeymoon?' Sophie felt faint.

'Of course. I want you to be my wife, Sophie. Not my mistress.'

Sophie felt her heart race, her lip quivering helplessly with joy. 'Are you sure, Dominic?'

His serious loving gaze left her in no doubt. 'I am not accustomed to saying things I'm not sure of Sophie. Surely you know *that* much about me by now? Will you marry me?'

This was one time when Sophie didn't have the slightest doubt about the answer she would give him. 'Yes, Dominic. I would love to marry you!'

It was hard to keep his elation hidden—and for once in his life Dominic didn't even try to hold back his emotions. 'Thank God for that! You know you would have destroyed me if you'd said no?'

At the mere idea that she could hurt the man she loved and cause him untold pain Sophie felt quite ill. 'I would never do that to you, Dominic. Not in a million years! Although, would it be possible—I mean, would you mind—if we only had a very small wedding?'

She almost held her breath while she waited for his response. To her relief, he chuckled. 'Knowing your aversion to weddings, my love, I would not have expected your request to be any different. Of course... Whatever you want Sophie. Now, tell me what this new job of yours means.'

'It means that—if you wanted me to—I could give up my current post and take a few months off so that we can be together. And if I get the job in Westminster in six months' time—and it's been hinted at that I stand a very good chance—I could practically walk to work!'

As he let out a long slow breath, the crease between Dominic's dark blond brows disappeared. 'So...it was meant to be.'

'What was meant to be?' Allowing him to steer her firmly into his arms, Sophie smiled up at the contemplative expression on his handsome face.

'You and me. The fates have conspired to help us be together, so it seems.'

'You believe that?' Her big blue eyes awed, Sophie sucked in her breath.

'I am beginning to believe many outlandish things since I have met you, Sophie darling!'

And before she could say another word to delay the thing that he most wanted to do, Dominic brought his lips down onto hers and kissed her soundly...

If you enjoyed what you just read,
then we've got an offer you can't resist!

Take 2 bestselling
love stories FREE!
Plus get a FREE surprise gift!